"My Dear Amalie, the Warning You Are Trying to Give Me— Is it That I Might Break My Heart Over You?"

She laughed ruefully. "No indeed, Major. I do not flatter myself so much. You want my body, true, but you have no heart to give me, therefore no heart to break. All I warn you is that your flowers, your dinner and your diligence may be sorely wasted. The man who keeps me has my fidelity."

"Does your—er—keeper object to your having men as close friends?"

"No. Surprising as it may seem to you, he trusts me. Are you offering me friendship, pure and disinterested, Major?"

"If it is all I can have, for the present, yes, I am, Amalie."

"It is all you can have—ever, Major."

"Time will tell . . ."

Dear Reader,

We, the editors of Tapestry Romances, are committed to bringing you two outstanding original romantic historical novels each and every month.

From Kentucky in the 1850s to the court of Louis XIII, from the deck of a pirate ship within sight of Gibraltar to a mining camp high in the Sierra Nevadas, our heroines experience life and love, romance and adventure.

Our aim is to give you the kind of historical romances that you want to read. We would enjoy hearing your thoughts about this book and all future Tapestry Romances. Please write to us at the address below.

The Editors
Tapestry Romances
POCKET BOOKS
1230 Avenue of the Americas
Box TAP
New York, N.Y. 10020

French Rose

Jacqueline Marten

A TAPESTRY BOOK
PUBLISHED BY POCKET BOOKS NEW YORK

Books by Jacqueline Marten

English Rose
French Rose
Irish Rose

Published by TAPESTRY BOOKS

An *Original* publication of TAPESTRY BOOKS

A Tapestry Book, published by
POCKET BOOKS, a division of Simon & Schuster, Inc.
1230 Avenue of the Americas, New York, N.Y. 10020

ISBN: 0-671-52345-7

First Tapestry Books printing September, 1984

10 9 8 7 6 5 4 3 2 1

POCKET and colophon are registered trademarks of Simon & Schuster, Inc.

TAPESTRY is a trademark of Simon & Schuster, Inc.

Printed in the U.S.A.

To a quartet of nonconformists:
My sisters, Cherie and Stephanie,
My brother Elliot.
And above all, my husband, Al.

Acknowledgement

To Kate Duffy,
who talks straight
but understands convoluted proposals

Author's Note

Due to its occupation by the British, New York was the center of military intelligence for the American side during the Revolution. There was no Triple Ring or "woman spy 103," but their true counterparts existed and performed even more heroically.

Spelling during the eighteenth century was phonetic, even among the educated.

Chapter One

New York, September 1776

A most horrid attempt was made by a number of wretches to burn the town, in which they succeeded too well . . . Many were detected in the act, and some killed upon the spot by the enraged troops in garrison.

—Sir William Howe in New York
to Lord George Germain in London

HIGH ON THE HEIGHTS OF HARLEM, GENERAL George Washington and many of his soldiers watched with grim satisfaction as rapidly-spreading fires etched a blazing skyline portrait of the destruction of Manhattan Island. Vast funnels of smoke spewed over the newly-gained Tory stronghold, while through the ranks of the New Englanders there were mur-

murings about God's help in laying waste the enemy-held city of New York.

A Connecticut sergeant spoke up for those who, if less reverent, were more forthright. "I misdoubt," he commented wryly, "that the Lord worked alone. A number of stout patriots must have helped Him."

The sergeant would have been elated to learn that below in the burning city, the British, particularly General Sir William Howe, were much in accord with his theory. No military mind could accept the coincidence of so many fires starting in so many distant places all at the same time. No, damn their rebels' hides, this was part of a dastardly American plot to destroy the rich harbor city, which the British had held only one week.

In the chaos and confusion of that hellish September night, the grim-faced British knew that, without a mighty effort, there might be nothing left of the city to hold. Without so much as a single gun's being fired, they might well suffer the defeat of losing New York.

Troops already quartered in the town and sailors, rowed over from British men-of-war in the harbor, labored tirelessly through the night trying to save people and buildings from the blazing inferno, emptying hospitals and jails of their wretched inhabitants and seeing to their transport. They fought an almost futile battle against the existing fires and mounted a monumental campaign to curtail the spread of the conflagration. As they struggled, they dealt as well as they could with the inevitable panic and looting.

As the hours went by and the enormity of the disaster became more evident, the rage of the military increased in proportion to their efforts and those suspected of complicity in the arson were dealt with on the spot, sentenced solely by the will of the weary, vindictive fire fighters. Matches in the hand or possession of combustibles were judged a sure sign of guilt. There was nothing to choose between revenge killings or miscarriages of justice. The inevitable mistakes would be buried, not corrected.

Jacob van Raalte, widower, merchant, and loyal servant of His Majesty King George, had been dining with friends near King's College when the first alarm sounded. He was a man of some standing in New York, much more important than his appearance proclaimed, for he was short and pale and pock-marked. He had a pronounced stoop, a shambling walk, and—unless he spoke slowly and with deliberation—a painfully obvious stammer. He had walked taller and prouder, in the way of the rich and the powerful, until one short year before. Then, a group of the Sons of Liberty—actuated, many said afterward, as much by envy as by patriotism—had punished his loyalist zeal with a rail ride around his once-beloved city.

Stripped of his clothing, shorn of his pride, his private parts most cruelly punished on the jouncing ride, Jacob van Raalte had never walked quite upright again or talked with his old easy assurance.

Now, as he whipped his horse along, forcing it in the direction of his Georgian mansion on the Mall near the worst of the fire, he spared only a passing thought for his two ships at wharf and his warehouses in lower Manhattan. They might all be gone, swallowed up in the flames, but so long as Melrosa was safe. . . .

"Melrosa." He said her name aloud on a sob. His adored youngest daughter, home alone with only the new housekeeper for protection. She could have been safely away from the city now, gone on a visit to Trenton along with Amalie and Julianne, but on the morning set for their leaving, she had awakened with a slight fever.

Seeing the stark terror on her father's face—for his wife Solange's last illness had started with a slight fever—without so much as a murmur of protest, Melrosa had relinquished her long-planned journey.

Never was there such a loving, thoughtful daughter—and now, because of his fears, she might be far more endangered than by a simple fever.

A quarter-mile from the van Raalte mansion a wild pig dashed into the path of Jacob's horse, which, already crazed with fear, reared up wildly, throwing him. When he overcame his daze and struggled to his feet, the horse was long gone and out of sight. The pig had stayed and was pawing at him menacingly; he had to threaten it with his whip to drive it away.

Dizzy, staggering, he continued along his way, ducking flying embers, watching indifferently as looters smashed through store fronts and bow windows and made off with valuables, hardly blinking when a soldier came running and, with a single shot, brought one fleeing man down almost at his feet.

He saw the blood bubbling from the mouth of the victim, who had fallen in an untidy sprawl still clutching a brass candlestick in one hand and a music box in the other. There might be looters breaking into *his* house! And she, his precious jewel, unprotected.

"Melrosa!" Jacob sobbed out again and stepped across the dead man.

The crooked, cobbled streets of New York were particularly hard for a lame man to traverse, but he struggled doggedly on—not seeing or hearing or aware of anything except his goal.

The great Broad Way was reached, and he took heart that Number 1, the Kennedy house, and its near neighbor were unscathed. But a block away his own house was already engulfed in flames on either side. He rushed up the steps as fast as his legs permitted, through the smashed and open front door.

He stood in the smoky center hall shouting hoarsely, "M-M-Mel-rosa!"

She came running from the direction of the drawing room in a long white night shift covered only by a blue velvet cloak, barefoot, a mass of hair, red-gold in the light of the fire, hanging all about her face. For all she seemed a small, slight girl, she was sturdier than she appeared, for hugged against her chest was the small heavy money box which he kept always in the wall safe, and she was dragging along on its ornate frame the huge portrait of her mother that had hung over the mantel.

"Melrosa," he croaked thankfully, and hugged her to him.

"We had better get out, Papa," she reminded him almost prosaically.

"Of course. Of course." He relieved her of the portrait. "Mrs. Cutler?" he asked as they hurried towards the gaping door.

She frowned slightly at mention of the housekeeper.

"She woke me and told me to get out, Papa, even before the fire began in our house. It seemed to start all at once in several different rooms, almost as though it had been set. I think she had something to do with it."

Two red-coated soldiers burst through the open door, their jackets torn, their faces grimed, one's hair burned part away.

"*Rous!*" they barked in German, and then in heavily-accented English, "Go out!"

Melrosa and Jacob obeyed quickly, but a

moment after they went plunging down the steps of their house, the Hessian soldiers followed, calling out to them. Each was carrying a tied sheaf of faggots dripping with resin.

The Hessians' shouts attracted a third soldier, an English lieutenant of dragoon, whose singed eyebrows gave him an eerie, satyrish look. He suddenly vaulted through a broken cellar window and joined the four, eyeing the bundled faggots accusingly.

"Is this your house?"

"Yes," answered Jacob readily and without fear.

"You burned it?"

"Certainly not. I was visiting friends. My daughter was home with only the housekeeper."

"Your daughter fired it?"

"Are you crazed? She was ill abed."

"One of you filthy Americans piled faggots and set fires all over that house."

Jacob van Raalte drew himself up as proudly as his weariness and crippled body allowed. "We are loyal subjects of King George."

"Everyone in New York is a loyal subject of King George," sneered the lieutenant, "but you damned provincials are burning the city under us just the same."

Melrosa huddled closer to her father, still hugging the money box. As she sensed danger, they smelled her fear, and it seemed to inflame them.

"*Vas is das?*" One of the Hessians grabbed

the box from her and broke open the lock. His eyes lit up covetously at the sight of the hoard of silver coins and paper money. His companions licked their lips.

"Looters!" said the British soldier, and his eyes met the Hessians in an unspoken signal. "House burners."

"So." The Hessians nodded solemnly.

A shower of sparks sprayed over all of them as the roof of the van Raalte mansion caved in and the walls crumbled. Jacob van Raalte, diverted for a few seconds by the heartbreak of watching the collapse of the home to which he had brought his bride, never saw the blow that felled him, but he was alive and aware when his ankles and shoulders were seized, and he was swung back and forth, back and forth, to the merry accompaniment of "London Bridge is falling down, falling down . . ."

Then Jacob was falling down, too, tossed into the very core of the hot blaze. His guttural stammering scream was mercifully shortened by the falling timber that struck him across the head one second before his bride's home became his funeral pyre, but it would ring in Melrosa's ears forever.

She had fallen to her knees screaming, too, but screams were a common part of that awful, awesome night when New York burned. No one took any notice.

She never saw one Hessian make the gesture that asked, Shall we send her after him, nor the Englishman's spoken answer, "You crazed? Look at her!"

Her hair was seized close to the scalp, yanking her head back so they could look at the pale purity of her small oval face, lashes quivering over eyes that had closed against the horror.

"We've got a better use for this one," the dragoon gloated.

They cuffed the sides of her head when she started to scream again, and she became numb and docile as they dragged her some blocks away to a street already devastated by the fire and deserted by the fire fighters.

In a cellar hole surrounded by mounds of still-smoldering ashes, they tore off her cloak so roughly the strings cut at her neck. They spread the cloak out and threw her down upon it. Then they spread her out, too, with one each gripping an ankle to keep her legs wrenched wide apart while the third took his pleasure between them. As in a game, they kept changing places, taking turns at her twitching, tormented body until the sounds of horses and men were heard.

Swearing then, in both English and German, the soldiers emptied the contents of the money box into their pockets and scrambled away, leaving the huddled little body on the ground.

An elderly Dutchman on his way to Bowling Green to inspect the ruins of his home found her in the morning. She was crawling about in the debris, bruised and bloody and barely able to call out.

Twenty-four hours later a farm wagon rolled noisily past the fish pond and the rolling green lawns to halt at the door of Frederick De Lacey's Turtle Bay estate.

The driver looped his reins and came around to lower the wagon-back. The girl who was his sole passenger struggled up from a corncob mattress. Rejecting the driver's arm, she made the slow, painful descent from the wagon and the slow, painful ascent up the steps of Lacey Manor.

Frederick De Lacey had heard the commotion at his front door and came from his library to discover the cause. He was in his shirt sleeves, a long clay pipe in his hands.

"God save us! Melrosa!"

As he called out in shock, his pipe fell to the hardwood floor and broke into a dozen pieces. He was scarcely able to believe that this pale pinch-faced creature with blinking, pain-filled eyes was the gay, engaging girl who had picnicked on his grounds only a month before.

"Uncle Frederick." Her lips quivered; her teeth chattered in the travesty of a smile. Then she looked around vaguely. "Papa," she whispered. "Did Papa climb out of the fire?"

Frederick De Lacey moved towards her, his arms ready to embrace her. To his consternation, she shrank away from him, her eyes widening in terror, her hands held out to fend him off.

"Don't touch me!" she cried.

A woman servant was summoned to take her upstairs to the best guest room.

"Shall I light the fire, Miss van Raalte?"

"No! No fire!" she gasped. "I would like—if you please—to be alone."

As the door closed behind the servant, Melrosa van Raalte stood at the window, shivering uncontrollably.

This is only the beginning.

It began as an echo in her brain.

Then she heard herself saying the words aloud. "This is only the beginning."

With the labored movements of an aged, rheumatic woman, she knelt at the window, looking towards the lush lawns that sloped steeply to the river.

The clock in the hallway chimed eleven, and scarcely a mile southward in the British artillery park a scholar-schoolmaster turned soldier-spy went to his death, quoting a Roman philosopher.

Captain Nathan Hale . . . only the beginning.

Chapter Two

Aboard a British Troop Ship on the Atlantic, Autumn 1778

". . . pay particular attention to the movements by land and water in and about the city especially . . ."

—*General George Washington in memorandum of instructions to his spies in Manhattan*

ALMOST ANY BREAK IN THE TEDIUM ON THE two-month voyage across the Atlantic to America had become a welcome diversion for the British troops. When the overflowing pails of the ship's refuse were dumped over the sides, shivering soldiers had formed the habit in all but the vilest weather of congregating around the rails to take note of how many grayish-black fins sliced through the water toward the floating garbage and how speedily it was engulfed and devoured by the wide-jawed predators. Their officers—equally interested—made a wise pretense of not knowing their men held regular daily pools concerning the number of sharks who came to feed.

On an unexpectedly warm day in early March one such officer, head uncovered, his dark hair dampened and darkened with spray, strolled onto the deck at this morning marine mealtime, and was presented with the ludicrous sight of a score or more of upturned buttocks, the most prominent feature of the bent-over military, their heads hanging out-of-sight over the rails.

He was about to withdraw discreetly when he noticed one bottom, plumper than the rest, attached to a pair of short legs, which had lifted perilously high above the deck and over the rail, in the eagerness of its owner to squeeze between his fellows and witness the sight below.

The officer took a quick step forward to yank at the back of the soldier's short scarlet jacket and bring him back to firm ground.

"Hey, you bas—"

The soldier choked off in mid-word as his slanting hazel eyes took in the gorget at the throat, the red sash, and above all the gold epaulettes on the broad shoulders that proclaimed a staff officer. His complexion turned the carroty color of the hair poking out from under a crested light cap. Then he came quickly erect, gave a smart salute and a gulped, "Sorry, sir, I thought—"

Standing tall above him, Major Alexander De Lacey surveyed the corporal, his straight black brows slightly raised. He should have recognized the buttocks as belonging to Mac-Dowell, the stocky young Scotsman who had made himself obnoxious to the rest of the troops all during the voyage by failing to succumb to seasickness even once and commenting on it continually to others less fortunate than himself while he stuffed himself with his own rations as well as theirs.

A voice at the end of the rail shouted exultantly, "Eight of the beasties, I win."

The corporal squirmed slightly, and Major De Lacey's brows descended to their normal position on his forehead. "Don't think," he admonished gently. "And, Corporal . . ."

"Yes, sir?"

"In the future, keep your feet planted firmly on the planking of this vessel . . . unless you are planning to offer yourself as dessert for those creatures below?"

"No, sir."

"Dismissed, Corporal."

"Yes, sir, thank you, sir," said the soldier in tones of such fervent gratitude that Major De Lacey could not hold back a smile as he proceeded below deck.

A few days later the Major and MacDowell

14

had another encounter. The corporal was standing at the ship's rail again, this time standing very straight with his feet in their heavy boots set solidly on the deck. Only his face appeared odd, with his mouth pursed up in the thick-lipped pouting look of a flounder as he sniffed doglike at the freshening breeze.

"Something wrong, Corporal?"

"No, sir. I was just wondering, sir, what caused that peculiar smell."

Major De Lacey took several short rapid sniffs himself, then suddenly a deep prolonged one. "Land ho!" he announced elatedly, a smile breaking up his rather austere features, giving him a younger, boyish look. "That peculiar smell is cedar smoke, Mac-Dowell, the pervading aroma of Manhattan Island. I would say that we were not more than—oh, perhaps forty miles from New York Harbor."

"Is that how New York smells, sir?" Corporal MacDowell asked with interest. "Like cedar smoke?"

"Very much so, and the odor will grow much stronger as we get closer. New York also carries the whiff of spices and rum plus fish and rotting sewage, depending on where in the city you chance to be."

"You've been there before, sir?" asked Mac-Dowell in the easy way so typical of a Scot, who, unlike an English soldier, considered himself the equal of any man.

"Briefly." Major De Lacey's eyes narrowed as he stared at the distant horizon. He seemed to be talking half to himself. "I was on duty with the King's Own in '76 when we fought at Long Island, where I was wounded. After a few months in hospital in the city I was shipped back to England, transferred to the War Office for—"

He came out of his reflective mood all at once and stared down from the advantage of his far greater height at the shorter, burlier soldier.

"Are you interested in the story of my life, Corporal?" he asked half-humorously, tipping back his hat and disordering his dark brown side curls.

"Yes, sir. I mean, no, sir. Only if you wish to tell it to me, sir."

The respectful voice was contradicted by the sparkling impudence in MacDowell's glinting eyes and the unabashed grin on his face.

Just for a moment a responsive sparkle lit up the Major's rather cold gray eyes. "I am going to be attached to the New York headquarters of Sir Henry Clinton. Does that information satisfy you, Corporal?" he asked gently.

"Attached to Command Headquarters, *yes, sir!*"

"I can't tell you how your interest and approval warm my heart, MacDowell."

This bit of satire was lost on the Scot, who

continued to grin cheerfully as he waited for dismissal.

Permission to leave granted, he saluted and wheeled about, only to be stopped by the icy voice of a British officer, uttering a brief command. "Corporal MacDowell, pray return."

Six-feet-two inches of lean hard British officer took a lofty, leisurely survey of five-feet seven inches of corpulent Scots corporal. Then, "How much did I win you, MacDowell?" asked Major De Lacey softly.

"S-s-sir?"

"The bet about my appointment. How much did you win?"

"Sir," answered the corporal in apparent shock, "betting is—"

"I am fully aware what betting is," Major De Lacey interrupted suavely. "Since mine is a guess, unsubstantiated and lacking evidence, you may answer without prejudice."

MacDowell hesitated. "Major De Lacey, sir, I am no' quite sure what *without prejudice* means."

"In this case," answered the Major easily, "that your answer will not be held against you. In fact, your answer will be quite forgotten."

"Oh, in that case, sir," said the soldier, unabashed, "a full guinea."

"My congratulations. I am happy to—er— have been of such service. However"—his voice hardened—"this is the last time my

17

memory will be so convenient; you take my meaning?"

"Aye, aye, sir," grinned MacDowell.

"Corporal," the Major reminded him freezingly, "we may be still at sea, but we have not yet changed our branch of service. Would you care to amend your answer?"

"Yes, sir. Thank you, sir."

Two hours later a knock sounded at the door of the coffin-sized cabin where Major De Lacey was awkwardly attempting to pack the two portmanteaus lying open on his bunk.

"Come in," he called impatiently, turned his head, then lifted his heavy dark brows in their habitual expression of ironic inquiry as MacDowell sidled sideways through the door and stood against the wall.

"I have my captain's permission to speak to you, Major, sir," MacDowell said defensively.

Major De Lacey balled up a soiled shirt and tossed it into the smaller of the portmanteaus. "I don't doubt it, Corporal," he said wearily. "What do you want?"

"I understand your batman's arm is so badly shattered, sir, you are sending him back on the ship for the return voyage to England."

The Major straightened. "Do I detect a note of censure, MacDowell?" he queried softly. "I am not planning to cast him adrift on the streets of London, you know. Once he recovers he will be given employment for which he is fit on my father's estate in Derbyshire."

18

"I felt sure you would do the right thing by him, sir," said MacDowell stolidly.

"As always," said the Major sardonically, "I am unmanned by your approbation."

"Thank you, Major." The corporal refused to be put out of countenance. "What I wanted to know, Major, sir, regarding your batman, would you be willing to get me transferred to take his place?"

"You!" thundered the Major. "An impudent, independent, cocky, self-opinionated Scot like you suddenly wants to be batman to a bloody Britisher!"

"Not to any bl—to any Britisher, sir, but to *you*, yes, sir."

"Why?"

MacDowell swallowed, then said with disarming simplicity, "I think we would get along together, Major."

"Would we, indeed! And what is your experience as a batman, Corporal?"

"None, sir."

"None?"

MacDowell smiled engagingly. "It means no bad habits to be broken of, sir," he pointed out.

"And your qualifications?"

"I'm a good forager, sir, you'll never find a better. I'm honest, thrifty, hard-working, loyal, and cannier than any Eng—regular soldier. I can no' play the pipes, but I'm a rare fine fiddler," he continued without false modesty. "I cook as good as any grand French chef, and I know all manner of useful domestic matters."

"For instance?"

"Well, for instance, sir, that you've made a sad botch of packing your portmanteaus, unless you like your jackets creased and your breeches wrinkled. If I might, Major De Lacey?"

The Major stood aside. "By all means."

Ten minutes later MacDowell was buckling the straps of the cases, both neatly and competently repacked.

"Thank you, Corporal."

"My pleasure, Major." MacDowell looked up at him expectantly.

"Tell me about yourself," Major De Lacey ordered abruptly.

"My father was in the ranks, sir, and my grandfather before him, though not by any choice of his, sir." His grin this time was without his usual humor. "He was in the '45 uprising, grandfer—captured a good bit after Cumberland wreaked his vengeance on the Highlands—so instead of immediate hanging, he was given his choice between the scaffold and taking the king's shilling. He was none so sure which was worse, but I'm told my old granny went down on her knees to him, so he chose the king. Of course"—an old bitterness crept into his voice—"the Scots who went to fight in Europe for German George left their women and bairns to starve. My granny did; my father did not. When he married, my mother followed the drum. 'Twas the only life I knew, so as soon as I was old enough, I took the king's shilling myself."

"I would not like to have a batman, however useful, who nourished hatred for the British," said the Major quietly.

"I hate some British but no more than some Scotsmen. A man's a man, and I've learned o'er the years not to judge him by which country he comes from. So long as I serve you, I'll serve you faithful, thankful to know that you'll treat me the same."

The Major looked down his long nose. "How do you know I will?"

"You said it yourself, sir. Your batman Sedley is no' being cast adrift on the streets of London. You're sending him home to your father's land. When I'm no longer fit to be a soldier, I have no mind to return to Edinburgh to starve. I feel better for my future knowing I will serve a son of the Earl of Beaumont."

"Second son," Major De Lacey reminded him. "Second sons do not inherit large estates."

MacDowell's eyes twinkled merrily. "I'm satisfied if you are, sir. I'm no' a very ambitious man."

The Major suddenly started whooping with laughter. "Nor I, now that I think of it," he observed presently, his gray eyes brimming with merriment. "In fact, it was a fault in me complained of by my teachers at Eton and frequently by my father."

He suddenly held out his hand. "I think you will be good for me, MacDowell. We have a bargain."

MacDowell thoughtfully regarded the unusual sight of an officer's hand held out to an enlisted man. After a moment he nodded his head and gave the hand a hearty shake.

"So we do, sir," he agreed.

Then he stepped back and saluted.

Chapter Three

New York, 1778

A performance of the Theatre Royal "for the laudable Purpose of raising a Supply for the Widows and Orphans of those who have lost their Lives in his Majesty's Service."

—*Public announcement in 1778*

"MAJOR DE LACEY IS HERE, SIR," THE COM-mander-in-Chief's military secretary informed him, then stepped back politely to admit the new arrival.

General Sir Henry Clinton eased his portly frame out of an oversized desk chair and came forward with both hands extended.

"Alexander, my dear fellow." A smile of delight erased lines of irritation from about his nose and mouth, giving his plump features a look of rare geniality. "Welcome to New York, my boy. How are you? Does the wound give you any trouble?"

"None at all, sir. I am perfectly fit, I assure you."

"And your dear father? Was he in good health when you left England?"

"In both his customary health and good spirits, Sir Henry, which is to say that he is able at all times to outride, outhunt, and outdrink both of his sons."

Sir Henry gave a brief bark of laughter. "That sounds like Lionel," he said reminiscently. "Don't be disheartened, Alex. He could always wear me out, too, in our heyday. Now back to you—are your quarters comfortable?"

"Most comfortable, sir. A very pleasant set of rooms overlooking the Hudson."

"Then I must ask you to excuse me for the present. I've another damned conference scheduled with some loyalist leaders to hear their unending complaints and demands. André will take care of you. You two are friends, I believe?"

"Since our unregenerate military beginnings with the Welsh Fusileers, Sir Henry. We were lowly second lieutenants together."

Sir Henry escorted the younger man to the door.

"Dine with me tonight," he invited abruptly. "A party of us will be going to the Theatre

Royal afterward. I have a box for the season. It's not London, my boy, but the best New York has to offer. I believe—yes, I am almost certain that André performs tonight."

Alex De Lacey grinned. "He always did love the sound of his own voice," he said with easy affection. "I hope his acting has improved?"

"Tolerably. Tolerably. You will see for yourself. If there is anything else I can do for you—"

Major De Lacey turned at the door. "There *is* one small matter, sir. My batman was injured aboard ship by a falling spar, and I am sending him back to Beaumont Hall. The replacement I have in mind is a Scots corporal who came over on the troop ship with me. His Brigade Major is reluctant to release him."

"A Scot, hey? Contentious creatures, the lot of them. Are you sure you know what you are about?"

"No, Sir Henry, I am not, but MacDowell assures me otherwise. He claims to be just what I require—loyal, hard-working, a fine cook, a good forager, smarter than any Englishman, and a great fiddler to boot."

"A fiddler!" Sir Henry's eyes lit up. Music, as De Lacey well knew, was his abiding passion. He himself played the violin and several other instruments. "I could use a fiddler for my orchestra; we're always short of men."

Major De Lacey bowed to his commander-in-chief. "I would be most happy to share MacDowell with you, sir. I doubt his duties will be too onerous otherwise."

"Give his name and regiment to my secretary. It will be arranged."

"Never doubt it," Captain John André confirmed to his friend a few minutes later, his eyes lit up with laughter. "In pursuit of a musician for his amateur orchestra, Sir Henry uses all the diligence, vigor, and determination that he is said to lack in chasing after the rebel army."

Alex De Lacey whistled. "As bad as that?"

André shrugged. "He never wanted the Command; all the army knows that. Every six months or so he sends in his resignation, and the ministry politely turns it down, even as it castigates him for not taking a more aggressive stance. This, he lacks the confidence to do, convinced he does not have a sufficient force to put down the rebellion. Our provisions, except those we get by raids into the areas around New York, must all come from England." He shrugged again. "So we stay here in Manhattan in a comfortable state of siege and—"

"And perform at the Theatre Royal?" Alex interrupted ironically.

"My dear fellow," André retorted, unabashed, "you know I always fancied myself as a Garrick."

"*I* know. Others at home do not. There has

been some furor about the questionable taste of British officers performing in public."

"Wait till they find out that British officers perform for hire," André told him callously.

De Lacey's eyebrows took a shocked leap up to his hairline. "You are not serious, John?"

"Quite, quite serious, Alex," André teased, his own eyebrows counterfeiting equal shock. "Oh, we frequently advertise our performances as being for the laudable purpose of raising funds for the widows and orphans of those who have lost their lives in His Majesty's Service, but the sad truth," he admitted cynically, "is that after we of Clinton's Thespians charge our clothes and carriages, meals and liquor against the theater receipts, the funds left for the widows and orphans is a trickle, not a stream."

He put his hand on De Lacey's arm. "You know as well as I, dear boy, that a British officer cannot live on his military pay alone, especially here in New York, where the barest necessaries are so dear. If one has not a private income like—"

Alex flushed slightly. "Like even a second son of the Earl of Beaumont?"

"Precisely." Having made his point, André smiled engagingly. "Myself, I think," he added airily, "that an officer's efforts to increase his income, by exertion of whatever talents he may possess, deserve the greatest encouragement."

Major De Lacey could not contain his look of

disapproval in the face of this sprightly insouciance. He burst out laughing. "You insufferable macaroni!" he exclaimed. "You haven't changed a whit since the days when you were torn between art and the military and your fair poetess."

"Oh, but I have, Alex. I am much more sober and industrious than my outward appearance conveys." Almost somberly he added, "As an aide to Sir Henry, and his close confidant as well, I do engage in politics and war as well as theatrics, I assure you."

It was easier to believe while he was speaking, unusually earnest in manner, than later that night, listening to him as he stood on the stage of the Theatre Royal, delivering a poem of his own composition.

Major Alexander De Lacey, friend of André since the start of their military careers, was wracked by such uncontrollable mirth during the recital, he was forced to make an abrupt departure from Sir Henry Clinton's box before his loud laughter could interrupt the performance and bring down the censure of his Commander-in-Chief.

In succeeding days De Lacey became aware that André was indeed a confidential aide to Sir Henry and very busy at headquarters during the day, deeply occupied with the theater during his free time.

His own schedule was much less busy. The duties he was given at headquarters filled no more than two or three hours out of the twenty-four and were largely devoted to billiards and bowling.

It was Sir Henry's daily custom, with an escort of his guards and favorites not on other duty, to go galloping madly along Broad Way each morning to one of the few gaming houses that had survived the fire of '76. After enough sport to satisfy him, the General would gallop back to headquarters past a hostile citizenry at the same reckless speed as before.

The rest of De Lacey's time seemed to be at his own disposal, and, though he had no inclination to act for either pleasure or for profit, he did spend a good many nights at the Theatre Royal, either attending dramatic presentations or listening to concerts, also arranged under the sponsorship of the cultured Sir Henry Clinton.

On horseback by himself he explored the city, north to south within the British lines, east to west from river to river, prowling about the wharves, occasionally coming upon quaint Dutch houses amidst the ruins and rubble and ashes of others destroyed in the fire. As spring weather took hold, he crossed by boat to the other islands about Manhattan.

Most of his evenings were spent dining and drinking with fellow officers, discovering the truth of André's assertion that even the barest necessaries were overly dear in New York.

After a few months, continuous pleasure-seeking palled; he was beginning to be bored for lack of occupation in the Occupation and uneasily conscious of a fount of stored-up energy that had neither outlet nor direction. Too fastidious to turn to the abundant camp followers and whores plying their trade in New York, only half aware he was doing so, he started casting about him for a mistress.

Chapter Four

New York, Spring 1779

Rivington is arriv'd—let ev'ry Man
This injur'd Person's Worth confess;
His loyal Heart abhor'd the Rebel's Plan
And boldly dar'd them with his *Press*.

—*Loyalist printer
Hugh Gaines
New York, 1777*

THE FIRST MONDAY IN MARCH, WITH SOME time on their hands, De Lacey and André decided to stroll from Clinton's headquarters to James Rivington's publishing house and print shop. André had promised to pick up the bound copy of a symphony by Haydn, which Sir Henry had ordered; De Lacey decided he might as well as not lay down a dollar for a box seat to the upcoming performance of *She Stoops To Conquer*.

Two other officers and some six or seven ladies and gentlemen of New York were busily turning over shelves of books and bound plays, studying paintings for sale, buying tickets, violin strings, or copies of Rivington's newspaper, *The Gazette*. They were no unusual sight, for since the publisher's return from England with an appointment as royal printer, his shop had become the crossroads of New York's cultural life.

A boy of about fourteen, having subjected a German flute to a minute inspection, put it to his lips and began to play a lively Irish air. At the end of his performance, he was rewarded with a lively burst of applause from the other patrons.

De Lacey alone did not join in the generous praise; his hands were clenched together too tightly, one against his gorget, one tangled in his sash. He had hardly heard the music, for which at any other time he would have clapped as heartily as the others. He had eyes and ears for only one person in the shop, no attention to bestow on anyone but the pocket Venus who stood talking to James Rivington at the far end of the counter.

Because of his own tallness, Alex De Lacey had always preferred a woman to be above average height, but that was all forgotten as he gazed in bemusement at the slender, shapely, deliciously small girl in her Watteau street gown of a heavenly shade of blue trimmed at the elbow sleeves and tantalizingly low, square-cut neckline with ruchings of creamy lace. A short silk capuchin of a much darker blue color lay open about her shoulders, hood thrown carelessly back, velvet ties dangling down across her bosom.

She wore her hair high enough to be modish without achieving the ridiculous. It was powdered to a fashionable white, with a side curl caressing each of her cheeks and two more cascading down her back. Her head was uncovered. She wore neither cap nor calash, which might, De Lacey speculated, be a tiny key to her character. She was in vogue without slavishly following rules of style, so she had a mind of her own, not just loveliness of face and form. There was pride as well as beauty in the lift of her head, the lines of her nose, the set of her alluringly full mouth.

The publisher had laid a half dozen volumes on the counter for her inspection, and she was poring over them with total absorption. Major Alexander De Lacey, studying the bewitching profile and the exquisite figure felt his heart turn over and his bones dissolve. In that moment he knew exactly why he had been so restless and unsettled. He knew precisely what he wanted . . . no, he corrected himself fervently, he knew *who* . . .

"Are you suddenly gone deaf, man?" André's voice seemed to be coming from a long distance off. "I have asked you three times—"

Visibly shaking himself free of his wandering fancies, Alex apologized.

"I beg your pardon, John, I was not attending. I was—tell me—" With a slight gesture, he indicated the enchantress at the rear of the shop. "Do you happen to know that lady's name?"

André said cheerfully, "Not only her name but the lady herself."

"Introduce me."

"I should warn you—"

"Present me."

It was so definitely a command; the rigidity of his face showed him so obviously past reasoning that André shrugged, lifted his eyes heavenward, then proceeded to oblige. De Lacey followed him down the narrow aisle towards the back of the shop, his sword knocking against his thigh and his heart against his ribs.

"Amalie, my dear, how good to see you again."

In a flash it passed through the brain of the infatuated De Lacey that the name was just right for her. This was no Sarah or Jane or Mary! As she turned quickly from Rivington to André, holding out both gloved hands and smiling in pure pleasure, he gave an audible gasp. She was even more beautiful face-to-face than in profile.

Her skin had the delicate translucence of porcelain even if the coral tint of her cheeks was not a gift of nature but had been acquired by artful use of paint and powder. Her nose, though far from being prominent as his own, had the same patrician length and strength. Her eyes, like her gown, were a heavenly blue, and the coquettish patch at a corner of her lips drew attention to the sensuous mouth.

André kissed both gloved hands, his peculiar rare grace combined with a half-mocking air that said, this is just a game and we both know it.

She sighed exaggeratedly, obviously playing the game herself. "La, sir, must you always try to flirt?"

"Trying," he retorted, "is as far as I ever get with you."

This could go on forever, De Lacey decided impatiently. Rivington might be content to hover in the background, smiling benignly; the Earl of Beaumont's son was not. He cleared his throat quite loudly, then surreptitiously dug an elbow into André's ribs.

Not surreptitiously enough, for even as André, beet-red from choked-back laughter, managed to gasp out, "I beg your pardon," the pocket Venus turned towards De Lacey, a discreet hand over her mouth belatedly attempting to conceal the amused quiver of her lips.

"Amalie, my dear, allow me to introduce to you—at his most ardent request—my friend Major Alexander De Lacey. Alex, may I present Madame Nostrand?"

Even as he bowed, De Lacey was reaching

for the fingers still resting delicately across her lips. He brought them to his own lips and kissed them so fervently, she felt the warmth of his ardor through the thin shield of her blue silk mittens and shivered a little, she hardly knew why.

This man spells danger.

Angry with herself for the sudden thought, she retrieved her hand. "A pleasure to meet you, Major," she said, her nod perfunctory to the point of rudeness.

He appeared not to notice. "The pleasure, the honor, and the joy are all mine, Madame Nostrand," he announced boldly.

She rolled her eyes towards André, as though questioning this excess of courtesy. "Major De Lacey has joined our staff at headquarters," he informed her.

"Indeed."

"He is quite frequently at the Theatre Royal," André went on.

She smiled quite graciously, her poise regained. "Then I shall likely see you again, Major De Lacey," she told him quite prettily.

"You may be sure you will," he promised her.

She turned back to the publisher. "Mr. Rivington, I have decided. This time I will take the book of *Loyal And Humorous Songs.* Perhaps next time, the others. Please put it on my account."

"Certainly, ma'am. Let me get you a fresh

copy. Ah, yes, here they are . . . I will just wrap it up for you."

"I have engaged a box for tomorrow night's performance of *She Stoops To Conquer*," De Lacey said as Madame Nostrand turned back to the two British officers. "I would be delighted if you would consent to join my party."

Across her powdered head, his eyes conveyed a question to the printer. He smiled when Rivington nodded and held up a sheaf of tickets.

"I thank you, sir," she said politely, "but I am already engaged for tomorrow night's performance."

"Another night perhaps? May we set the date now?"

"I am sorry, but I am not a spectator when I attend the Theatre Royal. My vantage point is never a box in the audience."

"I beg your pardon," he said in some confusion.

"I am—did not André tell you?—an actress. You will see me at tomorrow night's performance—on stage."

An actress. His heart started thumping against his ribs in the same pleased anticipation as before, only this time with more confidence. Not a lady, after all, but an actress.

Madame Nostrand accepted her wrapped book from Mr. Rivington with a brief word of thanks and moved towards the entrance to the street, the two men following her.

André appeared pensive, but De Lacey made no effort to conceal his manifest high spirits. His prospects seemed suddenly bright and the lonesome drinking nights a thing of the past. Unless she were aiming very high indeed, she could not hope to do better than one of Sir Henry's staff officers, particularly a son of the wealthy Earl of Beaumont.

"André told me nothing, but I should have known"—he bowed gallantly—"that so lovely a lady had to be something out of the common way."

They were on the street now. She turned to face him directly; there was no mistaking the contempt in her voice.

"You are under a misapprehension, sir."

He stiffened. "Ma'am?"

"I am nothing out of the common—for an actress," she told him sweetly. "I am also—Captain André could have told you that, too, sir—unavailable."

An open carriage rolled up and stopped in front of her. Disdaining their help, she handed her package to the driver and climbed up beside him, unaided. At her low-voiced instruction, the horses set off at a brisk trot.

Madame Nostrand sat with the book of *Loyal And Humorous Songs* lying on her lap, her back very erect. She did not once look back at the two officers standing out on the road in the path of a lumbering water cart, open-mouthed and speechless and in imminent peril of their lives.

Chapter Five

New York, Spring 1779

"... mix as much as possible among the officers and Refugees, visit the Coffee Houses, and all public places ..."

—*Gen. George Washington in memorandum of instructions to his Manhattan spies*

HALF AN HOUR AFTER THEY HAD DIVED OUT of the way of the water cart De Lacey and André sat at a small table in the coffeehouse which the enterprising Rivington—who never missed an opportunity to turn over a tuppence —operated especially to draw British officers.

"You have to understand, Alex," André was explaining with weary patience, the same ground having already been thrashed over, "this is America, not England. Different standards apply here."

"Americans are principally of British stock. You are not going to tell me that an actress is regarded here as a lady?"

"Not a lady in the English sense of the word," André said hesitantly, "but definitely —well, lady*like,* and definitely"—he eyed his friend with some belligerence—"to be treated like a lady."

De Lacey snorted his disbelief. "You called her *Madame* Nostrand," he said presently. "A courtesy title, or has she a husband?"

"She is a widow."

"Ah."

"Genuinely a widow. As a matter of fact, she makes no concealment about her husband's having been with the rebel army. She came back to New York only after he died in '77 in the fighting at Germantown."

"Was she an actress before her marriage?"

"Far from it. She belonged to one of the first families in New York. Her father was Jacob van Raalte who was killed during the great fire in Manhattan. He would have been as aghast as any English gentleman to see his daughter performing on a public stage."

"It was necessary to support herself? She has no family?"

"Sisters, I believe, and some relations in the

Jerseys, but she is an independent creature and really enjoys the theater life for itself." He grinned. "There are many of us who do, you know."

De Lacey ignored this jocular aside.

"You two played the game of flirtation like two old veterans," he pointed out.

"So we do, and so we are; but that's all it is, Alex—a game. If it will prompt you to cease dashing that stubborn Beaumont head of yours against a stone wall, however, I will tell you what I tried to explain an hour ago. Amalie Nostrand is—well, *taken*."

"Taken?"

"She has a protector."

"Who is he?"

"I don't know. I doubt that anyone does. Probably some older respectable citizen, perhaps a married man. He keeps very much in the background, probably for his reputation's sake; but he certainly provides a most commodious lodging for her in a house about two blocks from John Street, near the theater, which he visits discreetly and apparently not too often. She has a servant, a carriage—you saw it—rich clothing and jewels that no salary at the theater Royal could ever provide. She repays him with, other than the obvious, extraordinary loyalty and fidelity. In that her code of honor is as scrupulous as any man's."

"How do you know?"

"For God's sake, Alex, you have been panting after her like a stallion in heat since the first moment you set eyes on her. Did you doubt it was the same for many other officers loose in New York to dice and dally and drink and play at love? They make no bones, many of them, about how their hopes were cut up and *they* were cut down. The lady's tongue, you may have noted yourself, can cut quite sharply."

"I noted it," said De Lacey pensively. "It should lend a bit of spice to the chase."

André threw up his hands. "Be damned, you're impossible." Then suddenly his smile had his usual practiced charm. "You know, Alex, I hope the lady cuts *you* down to size; I think it would be vastly good for your character, you arrogant son of a lord. I shall watch the proceedings with great interest."

"Do so," De Lacey said amiably, threw down some coins on the table, and went off to buy a large basket of flowers for Madame Nostrand to be delivered to her at the Theatre Royal.

From that morning on he bombarded her with a daily floral tribute in containers ranging from the first modest basket to crystal vases and Wedgwood bowls. Included in each offering was his calling card, without any additional signature or flourishes.

He attended every evening performance in which she appeared, sitting in a box so near the stage, there was no way she could miss the frequent sight of him, especially when he stood to join in the cheers and applause at curtain's end.

Wise in the ways of pursuit when the quarry was female, however, other than the flowers and his attendance, he did not make the usual anticipated moves in the game. For more than a week after their abortive meeting in the print shop he did not press for a personal encounter. He neither came to her dressing room nor appeared suddenly when she exited the theater. He did not seek information—careful questioning of her own confirmed—from either her carriage driver or her maid. He made no attempt at all to see her offstage or to speak with her.

Prepared to rebuff him, her rebuff was not required.

This one was smart, Amalie told herself when a full eight days had passed. On the ninth morning, as she held an exquisite porcelain bowl of hothouse flowers in her suddenly icy hands, she found herself shivering as she had at their first meeting.

The thought flashed through her mind again as it had before . . . *this man spells danger* . . .

She had learned not to mistrust her own sure instincts and judgment. All day long the feeling persisted; so strong an inner message was not to be lightly dismissed.

On the ninth night she made her entrance on stage in *Othello* and glanced quickly up at the box she had come to regard as his. It was entirely empty and remained so all through her performance.

But he was there in the audience, she knew it, somewhere in a more distant box or even the pit. She could sense his presence all around her, smell it, taste it. He had rented the entire box, she was aware in the depths of her being, so that it would remain empty all night, serving as both a taunt and a reminder.

Damn him! Damn him! Did he think he could so easily put her off her stride? Two could flaunt as well as one, as she would demonstrate this night. And so she did, playing the role of Desdemona with such heart-wrenching emotion that all who saw her performance swore they had never before seen it enacted so brilliantly, not in London or in New York.

After the applause and accolades had died away, she went to her dressing room and lingered there, avoiding the other actors. The theater was empty and almost dark when she and her maid went out through the rear door to her waiting carriage.

Major Alexander De Lacey was there at the curb, his hand casually resting on the horse's neck of a hired hack that was standing in back of her own carriage.

He made her a sweeping bow. "Madame Nostrand, you were magnificent."

She inclined her head with studied stateliness; they might have been in some fashionable drawing room. "I thought you might say so, sir," she told him quite affably.

He laughed in genuine appreciation. "You knew I was there."

"I knew."

"Shall we go to dinner, ma'am?"

She drew on the long velvet gloves which she had been carrying in her hands. "Why, certainly, sir, it would be a vast pity to waste the fine meal you have already ordered."

As he laughed again, she turned to her maid. "Take the carriage home, Kitty. You may expect me in"—she turned her head to smile in inquiry at De Lacey—"an hour and a quarter, perhaps?"

"Two hours at the very least," he insisted firmly. "A good meal is not to be hurried, and some minutes must be allotted for the traveling distance."

Amalie smiled up at him with sweet insincerity. "But surely, sir, we are going to the Shakespeare Tavern, which is no distance away at all, either from here or from my lodgings?"

Without waiting for his reply, she turned back to her maid. "An hour and a half then, Kitty," she conceded. "Please wait up for me; I will be no longer." They both knew these last words were spoken for his benefit, not the maid's.

Inside the hired carriage he turned to her, his fingertips stroking the velvet-covered hand lying between them on the seat. "Why were you so sure our dinner was to be at the Shakespeare Tavern?"

She removed her hand from his, placing it on her lap while a darkling glance of her eyes flashed a warning that he attempt no other familiarity. "I have dealt with British officers before," she said in a tone of calm contempt. "You are, perhaps, less predictable than most but nonetheless somewhat predictable."

He suspected she was deliberately baiting him, trying to rouse his temper. If so, he was forced to acknowledge to himself, she was having no small success.

"You prefer American officers, perhaps, madame?"

"American or British, the tendency is the same. I find it to be a fault of your sex, sir, not of your nation," she returned politely.

"Did that include your husband?"

She turned a little away from him. The cool, cutting voice softened slightly. "My husband was a boy, Major. He died, poor lad, before he got to be a man." She shrugged. "I doubt not his manhood, had he ever achieved it, would have included all those other trying little traits of your sex."

"Such as predictability?"

"Boring, tiresome, and oh-so-typical predictability."

The amused contempt was back in her voice as she answered him. Another slight indifferent shrug accompanied each drawled adjective. He had a raging impulse to take her by the shoulders and shake her till her elaborate powdered headdress toppled about her ears and her entire mouth of pretty teeth fell out and she registered even a tenth of the emotion offstage that she radiated when she was on!

He had just clenched his own teeth together and folded his arms across his chest in a powerful effort at self-control when the carriage stopped. It was she who pointed out to him, "I believe we have arrived, Major."

He jumped out and handed her down, noting that her fingertips barely touched his proffered arm as they walked into the tavern. It was—predictably, as she had pointed out—quite cluttered with British officers, their ladies who were mostly not ladies, and some of the professional actors from the theater.

As they followed the manager to the private corner De Lacey had secured beforehand, hurrying past acquaintances and friends before they could be detained, he noticed the telltale smile quirking the corners of her lips and the familiar concealing gesture of her fingers laid across them.

His temper dissolved in a burst of genuinely amused laughter.

"Very well, Madame Nostrand," he acknowledged as they were seated, "one round to you."

Across the table his hard gray eyes sparkled

47

a promise that it would be her last round. She lifted her wine glass to him, accepting the challenge.

"That remains to be seen," she told him softly.

He lifted his own glass. "Your very good health, madame."

"I'll gladly drink to that. And to yours, too, Major." She took a few sips and set down her glass.

"*Madame* is so formal. Do you mind if I call you Amalie? It's a beautiful name."

"So my father thought. No, I don't mind at all. In fact, I prefer it. We actors are an informal lot, you know."

"But you have not always been an actor, have you?"

"Oh, come now, Major, I am sure you already know the answer to that question. You are a close friend of John André. I feel quite certain that you have ruthlessly pried from him any morsel of information that there is to be pried." She leaned back in her chair, faintly smiling. "I am here to tell you anything else you wish to know. There is no need of subterfuge. Feel free to ask your questions."

"Why did you choose the stage instead of living with your family?"

"My family, since my father's death and the wreck of our fortunes, consists of two maiden aunts now living in Jersey. They were dependent on my father and, after the fire, had barely enough to maintain themselves, certainly not me. In point of fact, I assist them."

"Your sisters?"

"They live with my Uncle Frederick, who is not really our uncle at all but was my father's closest friend from boyhood. His name is the same as yours, by the way, De Lacey."

"Could you not have lived with him too?"

"I could, but I chose not to. It would have been safe, sir, there's no denying that, but I dislike dependence, and safety at the price of boredom seemed too high a price to pay. Besides"—her face clouded over—"my sisters, *one* of my sisters did not approve of my way of life or my marriage. I could not live with her disapproval *or* her saintliness."

They were silent for a moment while a huge platter of shellfish was placed between them.

"The fact is," Amalie told him, breaking open a clam, "that I really enjoy acting. The stage is an end in itself. You must know, too—it is no secret among theater people— that I am no longer dependent on it for my income. I act now because I wish to; it is an exciting life."

"Now you sound like André. I think he would resign his commission tomorrow if the theater offered him any prospects as handsome as the army."

"I am sure he would. We are rather alike, he and I, which is why we understand one another so well."

"Is that supposed to convey some deep meaning to me?"

"Frankly, sir, it was more in the nature of a warning."

"You and André." He smiled indulgently. "I don't see even the slightest similarity."

"You would if you studied us more carefully, Major. Can you not see that we are both of us handsome, luxury-loving, excitement-seeking people with the care-nothing attitude of our Huguenot blood that no completely English person could ever understand? We will neither of us ever care for any other person quite so much as we care for ourselves."

He cocked a sardonic eye at her. "My dear Amalie, the warning you are trying to give me—is it that I might break my heart over you?"

She laughed ruefully. "No, indeed, Major. I do not flatter myself so much. You want my body, true," she said matter-of-factly, "but you have no heart to give me, therefore no heart to break. All I warn you is that your flowers and bowls—by the way, much as I appreciate them, I have space in my rooms for no more crystal or pottery—your dinner and your diligence may be sorely wasted. Even were my inclination otherwise, I *must* disappoint you. The man who keeps me has my fidelity."

"An admirable trait, fidelity," he said softly.

"I think so. In fact, one of my few virtues."

"Does your—er—keeper"—he saw with bittersweet satisfaction the deep flush that rose from her décolletage and swept up to the edge of her hairline—"object to your having men—like André—as close friends?"

"No. Surprising as it may seem to you," she returned his attack, savage in return, "he trusts me. Are you, by any chance, offering me friendship, pure and disinterested, Major?"

"If it is all I can have, for the present, yes, I am, Amalie."

"It is all you can have—ever, Major."

"Time will tell."

"Indeed it will."

"Will you be my friend, Amalie?"

"I think you would be a most—exhilarating friend, Major De Lacey."

"My close friends call me Alex."

"Then I shall, too, with the understanding, of course"—she speared a shrimp, dipped it into the sauce, and popped it between her luscious lips—"that our closeness is of the mind and spirit, not of the body."

While he watched her steadily, she lifted her wine glass again. "To friendship, Alex." Over the rim of the glass, her smile provoked, her eyes dared him to disbelieve her.

Chapter Six

New York, June 1779

Message in stain* to Benjamin Tallmadge of American Secret Service from Agent 103

". . . It is believed Rawdon will soon resign and Clinton's favorite John André will become his chief aide and head of intelligence. André secretly preparing list of prominent "Rebels" (names not secured yet) he has reason to believe may be won to British cause. He is also urging Clinton to a more brutal military prosecution of war . . ."

* invisible ink

DE LACEY STROLLED INTO ANDRÉ'S OFFICE, AN open letter in his hand.

"John, have you ever heard of an area in New York called Turtle Bay?"

André pushed aside a memorandum he had

been scribbling and casually covered it with a blotter.

"Of course, I have, and so will you, if this coming summer proves anything like the past."

De Lacey stared at his friend, a little perplexed by the edge of bitterness in his voice.

"I don't understand," he said.

"You will, dear boy, you will," André said with an airy wave of his hand. "Sir Henry uses a confiscated rebel estate at Turtle Bay as his chief summer retreat. Except for any minor foray he may choose to execute or order, I am sure he will summer there again. If he does, undoubtedly you—I, too, part of the time—will be a member of his entourage. A hell of a way to run a war, ain't it?"

Once again he seemed to shake himself free of his gloom. "Why do you ask?"

"This appears to be one of life's little coincidences, or rather, truth to tell, somewhat a large one. The first night I had dinner with Amalie"—he smiled reminiscently—"she mentioned that her sisters lived with an uncle, name of De Lacey too. Frederick De Lacey. Do you know him?"

"Of course—one of the more prominent loyalists and Clinton's friend. Their Turtle Bay estates almost match, but De Lacey's is far superior. He has the best stocked deer park and fish pond this side of West Chester and allows full rights in both to all of Sir Henry's staff. A bit straightlaced but a most pleasant and hospitable gentleman."

"Yes, so Amalie mentioned. Just out of curiosity, in my last letter home to my father, knowing vaguely that some of our family had come to the colonies about the turn of the century, I asked him if there was a connection. He knew of none himself, but he asked his cousin Henry, who is a walking genealogical history of our family on all continents. Listen to this."

He turned to an inside page of his father's letter and read aloud, "Henry tells me that my grandfather's youngest brother Lionel—I hope I was not named after him—the usual family ne'er-do-well, having exhausted his sire's patience in the matter of wine, women, and unpaid tradesmens' bills and gambling debts, was shipped off to America in the year 1703, with an annual stipend pledged to him, provided he remain on the wrong side of the Atlantic. A debtor's prison was promised to him should he be rash enough ever to return. The black sheep confounded everyone by going into the fur business in Canada and making a huge fortune, which he promptly increased by marrying money too. He fathered four or five sons. The eldest, Frederick, came to New York, where he, too, prospered in the shipping business. Frederick had only one son, and Henry presumes him to be the Frederick De Lacey you mentioned, who is, as far as he knows, a childless widower, about two-and-forty. He appears to have a manor house and farming estate in a place called Yokers or Yonkers, as well as a mansion in Manhattan, but he lives mainly at his New York residence in an area called Turtle Bay. Apparently a gentleman of substance. By all means, hold out the family olive branch . . ."

De Lacey folded the two close-writ pages of his letter and carefully placed them inside his jacket. "Impossible that it should not be the same man!" he told André. "I wonder if Amalie will visit there this summer, too."

"She never has, that I recall." André's forehead puckered up thoughtfully. "I seem to remember hearing of some quarrel between the sisters. In fact—"

He broke off, looking uncomfortable.

"In fact, what?" De Lacey asked him.

"I would rather not repeat what may only be idle gossip, Alex."

Alex snorted in derision. "Since when? You thrive on gossip."

"About people I am not attached to, perhaps," André admitted, "but in this case—"

De Lacey strode towards the door. "By all means, pander to your delicate conscience," he flung back over his shoulder. "I will ask Amalie myself; we are having supper tonight after the theater at the City Tavern."

"Alex?"

De Lacey wheeled around. "Yes?"

"I know I *said* that I would like to see you cut down to size by the lady but not to the extent that—fond of you," he explained, his voice apologetic, his manner oddly awkward for the graceful André. "I would not want to see you hurt, and I cannot see your father, or any of your family accepting her as a Beaumont bride—even for a younger son."

"Nor I," said Alex De Lacey grimly. "Yet I have never enjoyed a woman's company so tremendously and that without once being accepted into her bed. We are friends, John, even as you and I. We talk and we laugh together, commiserate when things go wrong; we are silent sometimes, yet even our silences communicate more than the empty chatter of dozens of girls in London and Derbyshire who I have dined and danced with and cannot even remember the names of."

"It might be wise to break it off sooner than later," said André uneasily, but De Lacey was not even listening.

"I hold her hand sometimes," he said half to himself, "her *gloved* hand."

"My friend, you are obsessed."

"Yes, I think I am," said Alex with the ghost of a smile. "You wanted me to be, did you not? You wanted my arrogance shaken and my pride laid low. Well, they have been almost since my first glimpse of her. She is an actress on the public stage, a provincial without family, the widow of a rebel soldier, and the paid

56

mistress of God-knows-who, and if any man dared name her not a lady, as I once presumed to do to you, I would throttle him with my bare hands."

"She is every inch a lady," returned André gently. "Think of her instead of yourself. If she cannot be *your* lady, might it not be wise to end the connection before *she* is hurt as well?"

"I am past being wise," said Alex gruffly, closing the office door behind him.

That night across the table at the City Tavern, as he cracked open lobster claws for her, he asked her straightforwardly, "Do you ever visit your uncle, Frederick De Lacey, at Turtle Bay?"

Amalie's body tensed; he thought she paled a little under the theatrical powder and rouge, but she answered quietly and directly, "Not for several years. Why do you ask?"

"I may be spending some time this summer at Sir Henry's Turtle Bay estate, which I understand would make me a near neighbor of De Lacey's. I was hoping you would be there then. We might have lovely rides together and some sailing, too, not just quick evening suppers. Also, I thought you might perform the introduction to my American cousin."

She had been staring down at her plate, her face tight and troubled, but at this she looked up quickly. "Your American cousin," she echoed.

"Yes." He took the folded letter from inside his jacket and for the second time that day read aloud the paragraph relating to Frederick De Lacey.

"Uncle Frederick will be overjoyed," Amalie assured him after her first exclamation of surprise. "He always had the intention of one day going to England and looking up his family connections. He will be so happy it happened the other way around, even if it took a war to bring you."

"You seem very fond of him."

"I am. He is the dearest man and has been very good to me and mine."

"Why then will you not visit him?"

She hesitated, her fingers tracing idle patterns on the table linen. "He is the dearest man," she said again, "but very high-principled. He cannot approve of—of many things I have done, the way I live. He—"

"Are you saying he would not receive you?"

"He would receive me," she said in a stifled voice, "but it would be to—to place him in a most embarrassing position. I choose not to do so." She propped one elbow on the table and lowered her face into her splayed fingers. "Besides," came her muffled voice from behind the hand, "there are other things—I am ashamed to tell you—you will find out soon enough if you go to Turtle Bay."

He reached forward and slowly, one by one, pried away the fingers from her face.

"Do not distress yourself, love," he said gently. "Let us talk of something else. Or," he suggested, as her face in no way brightened, "we can eat a great amount and never talk at all. Then we have a third choice, which is to skip the food but to drink a good deal. I have never seen you the worse for wine, my sweet. I am sure you would be delightful in your cups. Fourthly, we might—"

The smile he had been trying to coax from her blossomed into a full-bellied laugh. "Alexander De Lacey, you are a prince of fools," she flung at him across the table in the throbbing voice she used on stage to send her every word to the farthest corner of the theater.

People from the nearby tables turned around to stare. Once, not so many months ago, Alex De Lacey of the proud Beaumont family would have squirmed at being made so conspicuous. Now he was only conscious of a strong feeling of satisfaction in having comforted her.

Immediately he began to discuss the performance that night of Sheridan's play, *The Rivals,* so new to America. Further questions could wait until he arrived at Turtle Bay. He would write to Frederick De Lacey this very evening and send his letter by messenger in the morning.

Turtle Bay
21st June, 1789

My dear Major De Lacey:

I had Extraordinery Plesure in recceving yrs of the 20th. Although the History of our Family in England is such that our sons in ev'ry Generation have Served there Country in far-Flung corners of the World, still it struck me as a Wonderfull Twist of Fate that your Servise should have landed you allmost at my Doorstep. I greevously Regrett that many months have Passed with you in New York and I not Awaire of it.

It is in Intension to write to Sir Henry at Once to Beg the Indulgense of your Company whenever it can be Spared to me.

Believe me, my dear Cousin, whist you stay in America, my Home will be Allways your Home.

Yr. Hmble. Obdt. Servant,
Frederick De Lacey

Amalie read this letter in her dressing room between acts while De Lacey lounged against her dressing table, sniffing at her perfume bottles and getting in Kitty's way.

She smiled brilliantly as she handed the letter back.

"He really means it," she declared with confidence. "He would take in every friend, any family, all the strays and needy about, if the house would but hold them all. When will you visit?"

"Not till Sir Henry insists." He came up behind her, his hands resting lightly on her bare shoulders as he smiled into the square mirror at their joint reflection. "I shall not leave you till I must."

Kitty sighed and walked out of the tiny room.

Amalie's smile faded. She turned around on her stool to face him directly, her expression faintly troubled.

"But Alex, *I* must leave you, did you not understand that? Manhattan is a most unhealthful spot in summer. The wealthy leave for their summer estates along the rivers and up in The Bronx and West Chester. The higher echelons of the military do the same. The theater, as you know, closes next week. I shall go to Jersey, as I do every summer, until we reopen in September or October."

"I knew the theater was closing; I had not realized that you, too, were going away."

"Oh, yes." She turned back to the mirror, making great play of dipping two fingers into a rouge pot and smoothing spots of color onto her cheeks, all the while carefully avoiding his eyes.

"What is the great attraction of New Jersey?"

"My two aunts live there—near to Trenton."

"Ah, yes, the two dependent aunts. They are

your only reason," he asked ironically, "for a two- or three-month visit?"

Amalie's eyes met his in the mirror once again. Slowly she moistened her lips with the tip of her tongue. "No," she said baldly.

"I see."

He could detect her hands trembling as she put down the rouge pot.

"Your good friend?" he persisted mercilessly.

"Yes," she whispered. "His home is in Trenton."

"How convenient."

"Alex, please. It is no surprise to you. You always knew there was someone."

"I knew," he said violently, "but as long as you were with *me,* not with *him,* I could bear it."

The door opened and Kitty poked her head through. "Madame, it's almost time."

"I need just two minutes more, Kitty." The head withdrew.

"Alex, please try to understand."

His hands took hold of her shoulders again, but this time they gripped so powerfully, she grimaced in pain. He bent over to press his face against hers, bringing them cheek to cheek.

"Don't go to him, Amalie," he whispered, urgent and imploring both. "Stay here with me."

Before she could answer, his mouth found hers, but her lips remained cold and still beneath his. There was resistance in every line of her body.

He straightened up and moved away the better to look down at her. Her lips were quivering now; she was blinking back tears, but her face had gone strangely remote.

"Amalie," he said uncertainly.

"I want to be sure I understand you," she said in the hard, cutting voice of Madame Nostrand at their first meeting. "You want me to give up being *his* mistress and become *your* mistress instead. Do I have that correctly?"

He knew what she wanted to hear. *I want you to be my wife, Amalie.* He knew what he wanted to say to her. *Oh God, how I want you to be my wife, Amalie!*

In America, it might work . . . but in England. Oh, my God, in England she would be ostracized, ignored, outcast, and he, jeered at for even trying to win her acceptance.

"Amalie—"

But he had hesitated too long.

She twirled one of her errant side curls around a finger as though there was nothing more important on her mind than restoring its fullness.

"Forgive me for not being overwhelmed," she said in a flat, emotionless voice, "by the prospect of giving up a profitable certainty for the pleasure of becoming *temporarily* your mistress—until you go off to fight or return to England or find a whore whose charms you prefer to mine. I am afraid I must decline."

A knock sounded on the door. "You are needed on the stage, Madame."

"In all these months I have asked nothing of you beyond friendship," he hurled at her in a low impassioned voice.

She pulled off her dressing cape, walked to the door and flung it open.

"I have been awed and admiring of your patience," she said, her own voice low but so bitter it could have curdled cream. "The military strategy you employed has been nothing short of genius, but it was wasted." She flashed him her best actress' smile. "I take it, our friendship is over?"

"It is if you go to Trenton," he said evenly.

"Good-bye then, Major De Lacey."

He stood motionless outside her dressing room door, watching her all the way to the stage; she never once looked back.

Chapter Seven

Turtle Bay, August 1779

Sister, wrong me not
Nor wrong yourself . . .

—*The Taming of the Shrew*
William Shakespeare

AS A SERVANT LED HIS HORSE AROUND TO THE stables and Major Alex De Lacey climbed the broad stone steps of Lacey Manor, his host came forward, both hands outstretched. His round, ruddy face was wreathed in smiles; his blue eyes under the thick brows seemed almost childlike in their innocent delight.

"Welcome, cousin, welcome," he greeted the younger man with un-English warmth and exuberance. "This is a happy day for my house."

The Major bowed formally and replied with some slight disregard for the facts, "I am more than happy to be here, sir, and regret that my military obligations kept me from coming sooner."

The truth was that he had idled away much of the summer in Manhattan until André—returning from one of his brief mysterious trips to the north—informed him with the disagreeable bluntness of long friendship that he had mishandled Amalie shockingly, and it was time he abjured from such sulking.

"Come in, come in to the house, Cousin Alex. You do not mind if I call you so, I hope? We are, perhaps, a little less nice about social distinctions than you may be accustomed to."

De Lacey bowed again, more easily this time. The other's cordial informality was contagious. "I am honored to be so soon accepted as family, Cousin Frederick. Indeed," he added, thawing even more, "I must admit that if I met you in the middle of the American wilderness without even knowing your name, I would recognize you at once for a De Lacey. You are the very image of the third Earl, my father's father. He died when I was just a lad, but his portrait hanging in the great gallery at Beaumont could easily be mistaken for one of you. All that is lacking is a suit of salmon-colored brocade and a great curled periwig."

Frederick De Lacey laughed heartily as he ushered his guest into the drawing room. "Never say so to Julianne," he chuckled, "or I am liable to find myself not only wearing both but foolishly sitting to be painted. When the journeymen painters come by, she is always at me to have one of those great portraits made up to hang there over the mantel."

"It seems a reasonable desire, Cousin," Alex told him pleasantly.

"Not to me." Frederick De Lacey shook his head. "I have no wife to fancy herself delighted by a painter's flattery of my person, nor children to provide me posterity who will feel the interest you just expressed in family resemblance to an ancestor."

"Then the Julianne you mentioned is not . . ." With a show of delicacy Alex refrained from finishing the question to which he already knew the answer. His father's first letter had informed him that his host was childless; what he burned to know was whether this Julianne was Amalie's sister.

Frederick indicated a comfortable armchair and poured two glasses of wine from a crystal decanter on a side table.

"Julianne is not related to me by blood, though I call her niece," he said. "Her father, Jacob van Raalte, was my good and dear friend. Since his death Julianne keeps house for me. I would have preferred that she restrict herself to the role of daughter, but she was never one to be idle. Even now she is supervising the maids as they ready your bed-chamber."

"All is prepared, Uncle Frederick," said a soft voice behind them. "His portmanteau is unpacked, and if the Major wishes to wash, hot water is being fetched for him."

Alex De Lacey rose from the comfortable depths of the armchair as Frederick De Lacey turned, beaming, to perform the introduction.

"Julianne, my dear, may I present my long-awaited kinsman, Major Alexander De Lacey." He walked toward the girl standing in the center of the room, her shoulders a little hunched over, her head down so that all Alex could see of her was the snowy linen expanse of her Joan cap. There was something protective in the way Frederick put his arm about the drooping figure. "Cousin Alex, this is my dear ward, Julianne van Raalte."

The head came up, revealing a face that bore a superficial resemblance to Amalie's but was so inferior in every separate feature, he could almost feel a pang of pity for the girl. Her eyes, like Amalie's, were blue but of a much lighter shade and not nearly so large or lustrous. They stared at him from behind silver-rimmed spectacles, not with the laughing candor of her sister's but with a kind of critical coldness. Her complexion was sallow, her forehead and cheeks slightly pitted by pockmarks. Her nose began as the long, elegant feature that gave character to Amalie's face, then curved up towards the center and ended in too-wide nostrils. Her mouth was nicely shaped, but the lips looked tight and prissy.

"How do you do, Major? Welcome to Lacey Manor." Her words were all that was proper; her tone was not. She spoke in the same soft way that she had before, but her whole voice was cool and colorless and composed to the point of indifference.

Mannerless little prig, he thought, all pity forgotten, and said aloud suavely, "Thank you, *Cousin* Julianne. The warmth of your welcome is all I have been led to expect of American hospitality."

Quick enough to understand this excess of politeness for the rebuke it was, an unattractive flush overspread her face and neck. The smattering of pockmarks stood out even more against the mottled red, heightening her lack of attraction.

"I—I—" She cast a look of wild appeal toward Frederick De Lacey, who cocked his head rather quizzically at both of them as he handed her a glass of wine.

To the Major's astonishment she emptied it down her throat like a seasoned toper, all in one long gulp.

"I must beg your pardon, sir, and Uncle Frederick's as well. You did right, Major, to remind me that, in failing my duty, I shamed not just myself but my uncle's hospitality as well." Her head was bent again, her hands

69

clasped across her flat bosom. "I must ask you both to forgive me."

Alex found his own cheeks reddening; it had not been his intention to reduce her to a state of such gibbering abasement. Before he could answer, she set down her wine glass and dipped him a brief curtsey, her eyes fearful, her body braced, almost—nonsense, he must be imagining things!—as though she feared a blow or at the very least another rebuff.

"May I show you to your room, Major De Lacey?" she asked him anxiously. "And do you accept my apology, sir?"

"Yes, you may and yes, I do, on two conditions; one, that you cease being so da—blasted apologetic and two, that you stop sirring me. Call me cousin, if you will, as your uncle does."

"Yes, Cousin Alex, whatever you wish. Pray come with me, Cousin."

Sighing—the girl was utterly without humor!—he followed her out of the room.

As they climbed the narrow winding stairs to the second floor, he noted that Julianne's figure was light and pleasing—even in the sack of a gown she chose to wear—but by no means as curved and shapely as Amalie's. She was much the taller of the two but carried herself with less grace and confidence.

He studied her as she moved about the cheerful bedchamber, pointing out its amenities. True, she was not a handsome girl, but need she be so irritatingly unaware of her femininity? She was not a Quaker, so far as he knew. Why then, the drab gray Quakerish gown with its limp overskirt and unadorned bodice buttoned all the way up to her throat, the plain Quakerish cap tied under her chin and pulled so far forward that only the top of two mouse-colored braids skewered to the top of her head showed beneath it?

A sudden thought struck him. Was it possible that the constant and inevitable contrast with Amalie all through her girlhood had prompted her to retire entirely from the contest?

He said on impulse, "I believe I may be acquainted with your younger sister."

Julianne was on her knees beside his bed, one hand under the counterpane as she unselfconsciously smoothed out the featherbed beneath it. She looked up, astonished.

"You cannot know Melrosa," she told him frowningly.

"No, I meant Amalie. Madame Nostrand. Is she not your sister?"

Julianne rose hastily to her feet, forgetting the wrinkles in the coverlet. Her color was high again, her lips compressed.

"If being born to the same parents makes us sisters," she announced in the same tight, contained voice that had preceded her apology, "then, yes, we are."

What a scratchy female she was, to be sure! Alex thought wearily, not sure he wanted the trouble of trying once more to pacify her.

A knock sounded on the door, and Julianne jerked it open to admit a pert young maid bearing a heavy copper can of water. She set it down on the bedstand, curtsied, and departed. Julianne prepared to follow her, then turned suddenly in the doorway.

"And she is *not* younger than I!" she declared almost heatedly. "No matter what she may have told you, Amalie is two years the elder!"

"She told me nothing," Alex said gently. "It was just my own assumption."

Too late he realized this unfortunate bit of tactlessness was calculated to increase not to lessen her ire. With only one scathing glance at him—her manners once more forgotten—she rushed through the door, slamming it shut with enough force to rattle the glass in the window.

He had barely time to unbutton the top button of his jacket while reflecting that, homely or not, to be pitied or not, Miss Julianne van Raalte stood in sad need of a hand across her backside, when the door was flung open again. He groaned aloud. *Not* more apologies?

"We dine in an hour and a quarter," came an icy whisper through the opening before the door closed again, this time slowly, cautiously, quietly.

Chapter Eight

August, 1779

London Bridge is falling down
Falling down
Falling down
London Bridge is falling down
My fair lady.

Take the key and lock her up
Lock her up
Lock her up
Take the key and lock her up
My fair lady.

AN HOUR AND TEN MINUTES LATER, ALEX WAS directed by a housemaid, this one plump and middle-aged, to the dining room where the great round mahogany table was set for only three.

Frederick greeted him with his usual smiling warmth; Julianne with her characteristic chilling indifference. They had barely seated themselves when the same housemaid returned looking somewhat harassed. With a murmured apology, she came and whispered into Julianne's ear, then hurried away.

Julianne stood up, returning her folded napkin to the table.

"Please excuse me, Uncle Frederick—Maj—Cousin Alex."

Frederick De Lacey asked calmly, "Melrosa?"

"Yes. Mary says that she is—singing *Lon-London Bridge*." Alex looked up at her curiously, surprised by the quivering voice, the tremors shaking her body.

"Pray go on with your meal, gentlemen." She gave both men the ghostly travesty of a smile, then turned to face Frederick. "I shall probably be gone for some time, Uncle. It would be best if I have the kitchen send up a tray for me along with Melrosa's."

Frederick nodded his approval, then said calmly to the Major as Julianne fled the room, "I thought it would be pleasant to have just an intimate family dinner tonight so that we might all get better acquainted. I regret now I did not invite some other officers."

All! Alex's ears pricked up in alarm. Good God, that single small word included Julianne. Was his cousin by any change playing matchmaker? Could he possibly have that homely, prickly spinster in mind as a bride for even a younger scion of Beaumont?

Thinking to depress any such pretension right at the start, he spoke with distant civility. "I am pleased at the opportunity for *you* and *I* to become better acquainted, Cousin Frederick."

Not missing the slight emphasis on the pronouns, Frederick cast him a sudden piercing look from under his shaggy eyebrows. It reminded Major Alexander De Lacey that this was a man of stature and substance in New York. His cousin was far more intelligent than he appeared, and he himself had been thinking like a fool—a stiff-necked, prideful fool.

He waited till the maid who served the soup had left the room, then asked simply and naturally, "Is Melrosa the other sister?"

"The youngest." Frederick added softly, half to himself, "The sweetest, like her name, the honey rose."

"Is she ill, sir?"

"There is a summer storm brewing, I think. It tends to make her a little restless. She is—she has a somewhat nervous temperament."

Alexander waited politely for a moment, realized no further information would be volunteered and plunged directly into the matter closest to his heart.

"Madame Nostrand and I have spent much time together since my arrival in New York." Aware of another compelling stare from the bright blue eyes, he elaborated hastily, "André introduced us, and we three have had some very agreeable times. I dine with her alone after the theater twice a week, but regrettably there has not—I have not—she is—"

"I understand, Cousin."

"You do?" said Alex with some bitterness. "Then I fear you have the advantage of me, sir."

"I have known Amalie all her life," the other explained gently. "My own son died of the fever when he was three, and Jacob's girls have been the daughters I never had."

"What happened between them?" Alex asked him abruptly. "Julianne seems to hate Amalie. Did she always? Is it just female jealousy?"

"*Female* jealousy, indeed!" Frederick mocked him wryly. "I am afraid that denigrating phrase would find no favor with either of the two." He leaned back as his soup bowl was whisked away and a fish plate slapped down before him. "Say, rather, it is a quite human resentment," he continued more seriously. "Young Billy—that is to say, Amalie's husband, Lieutenant Nostrand of the rebel forces—was at one time affianced to Julianne. He was with the American army, and Amalie was visiting her aunts in Trenton, when it was captured by Washington's troops. A short time later we learned by letter from one of her aunts that Amalie and Billy had wed."

"She eloped with a man to whom her sister was betrothed!"

Frederick crumbled a chunk of wheaten bread between his fingers. "It does not sound nice, I admit," he began, "but—"

"Nice!" Alex De Lacey repeated the simple word in tones of loathing. "You express yourself rather temperately, sir," he said with suppressed violence. "I would think that—"

"But," Frederick interrupted firmly, "there were extenuating circumstances. We all knew Julianne had come to regret the engagement. Three times she postponed the wedding date. Amalie—after her father's death and the loss of his fortune—wanted a future with a husband. Julianne did not, but neither did she seem able to break off her betrothal. Possibly Amalie thought she was gaining her own ends and at the same time doing her sister a service—"

"You can't believe that, Cousin Frederick!"

"Perhaps not," Frederick admitted, "but I do understand that while Julianne dithered and delayed, Amalie recognized what she wanted and went after it. If her methods were somewhat less than honorable—poor lass!— she soon paid the piper. Billy was killed in a skirmish, and she was widowed six weeks after she became a wife, worse off than she had been before. His family recognized no obligation to assist her and she lost her sister and the home she might have had with me. Julianne's pride has always stood in the way of any forgiveness, and Amalie—who is not without enormous pride of her own—will not come here without it."

"I cannot blame Miss Julianne for disgust of her sister's conduct. I have thought many hard things about Amalie but never that she could be so grasping. And disloyal."

The American's face became somewhat rigid at the disdain in the Englishman's voice. "You must be one of the few righteous if you can only give your love where your object is worthy and deserving," he said with deceptive mildness. "Have *you* never been loved except when you merited it?"

"I love Amalie!" Alex burst out to his own surprised dismay. He had never intended to confess it. "And she is in Trenton—with her lover."

"Did you ask her to stay here with you?"

Alex's voice shook. The bitterness of her refusal was with him still. "I *begged* her to."

"And what inducement did you offer her?" Frederick asked with gentle but pointed irony. "By any chance, marriage, Cousin?"

Alex's eyes glazed over; his face grew pale. Like a schoolboy he used the tip of his tongue to moisten his lips. Like a schoolboy, he stammered out his excuses. "I am a Beaumont, sir. I have obligations to my name and family. Her past—her present way of life—so many circumstances combine to make it ineligible. You are a De Lacey, too, Cousin. Surely you— understand?"

"An *American* De Lacey," Frederick reminded him blandly. "My grandfather was thrown off by that same family to whom *you* owe allegiance. In this country, in our station in life—the one Amalie was born to no matter what she has since done or become—an honorable offer of marriage is expected to accompany a sincere declaration of love."

There was a moment's strained silence before Frederick's eyes lit up as he exclaimed aloud in satisfaction, "Ah, the roast duckling. Is not that a smell for the gods?" He rubbed his palms together, then, as the platter was set in front of him, picked up a wickedly sharp carving knife and tested the edge against his finger. "Wait till you taste the duck with Mrs. Wister's orange sauce, Cousin Alex. Sir Henry invites himself here often just for this one dish. Will you have a breast or a leg or perhaps a little of both? Pray help yourself to the asparagus; it is grown right here in my own greenhouse—as fine as any in England, your officers tell me."

Obediently Alex served himself from the asparagus dish and murmured his thanks as a generous portion of the duckling was handed over.

As he started to eat, he braced himself for a resumption of what he could only regard as polite hostilities.

Instead, Frederick asked him, "Do you play chess, Cousin? I have not had a game for some weeks."

"I am not as skilled a player as my father, but I usually manage to give him a good game."

"Excellent. A fine dinner, a glass of wine, and a challenging game of chess. What more could a man ask?"

The Major glanced at his cousin sharply. Frederick seemed genuinely to mean what he had just said. The subject of Amalie was apparently finished. Alex felt partly relieved, partly regretful.

Damnation, I must be besotted! he told himself. Or, as André had put it, obsessed. To want to discuss her so much he was even willing to court belligerence to do so.

The duckling *was* delicious, but his appetite had suddenly diminished. He was glad when the meal finally ended, and they left the dining room in favor of the small well-heated library where the chess game had been set up.

As they strolled across the hallway from one room to the other, Frederick stopped short and, in courtesy, Alex stopped with him.

A high, sweet, childlike voice was floating down from an upper floor.

> *London Bridge is falling down*
> *Falling down*
> *Falling down* ·
> *London Bridge is falling down*
> *My fair lady.*

Frederick went to the foot of the stairs and peered anxiously up. "Julianne," he called.

Her disembodied voice, soft but clear, carried down to the men in the hallway.

"It's all right, Uncle. I'm here with her. We walked a little; then she wanted to visit my room. She will be sleepy soon. I gave her some soothing herbs in her wine."

"You won't forget to lock the door?"

"No, of course not, Uncle Frederick. I have the key here in my pocket. Please don't fret. She is fine now." Her voice sounded farther away, but the words were distinct. "Yes, my little love, I am coming. There, here is my hand."

Soon the same sweet tremulous voice that had sounded before began to sing again.

> *Take the key and lock her up*
> *Lock her up*
> *Lock her up*
> *Take the key and lock her up*
> *My fair lady.*
> *London Bridge is falling down*
> *Falling down*
> *Falling down . . .*

The voice faded away into nothingness, and Alex looked at his cousin, curious and inquiring.

"I am quite looking forward to our game," said Frederick as he led the way into his library.

Chapter Nine

Yankey Doodle

Father and I went to camp
Along with Captain Goodwin
And there we saw the men and boys
As thick as hasty pudding.

Yankey doodle keep it up,
Yankey doodle dandy,
Mind the music and the step
And with the girls be handy.

THE ONE GAME BECAME THREE, ALL WON BY
Frederick but hotly contested until the very
end. Well satisfied with the evening's entertainment, Frederick bade his guest a warm
good night as he presented him with his candle set in a plain pewter chamberstick.

The Major reached the door of his room just

as Julianne came round the corner of the rear stairway leading from the third floor. She walked wearily, shoulders sagging. In the dim-lit hallway, her complexion looked more sallow than ever. Alex lifted his candle for a closer glimpse of the face so like and so unlike Amalie's. She had removed her spectacles—he could see them sticking halfway out of her apron pocket—and her eyes were puffy and red, either from weeping or perhaps too much sewing or tambour work by candlelight.

"You look tired, Cousin Julianne," he said with easy sympathy. "It has been a long day for you. I hope," he added conventionally, "my visit has not given you too much extra work."

She replied to this commonplace courtesy in her typical deadly earnest manner. "No more than any other guest, Maj—Cousin Alexander. I am quite used in the summer months to having Sir Henry's officers constantly here for our cookery and sport. Indeed"—she smiled wanly—"to have only one of you is restful. Tomorrow there will be a half dozen more."

"Good night then, Miss Julianne," he told her in some exasperation.

"Good night, Cousin Alexander." She opened the door to the room adjoining his. "As you can see, I am close by. If you need anything, just tap on my door."

He bit back the suggestive remark which most probably he would have made to any other woman in the world but this sexless, humorless, unaware non-woman. It would not do to throw her into screaming hysterics or those awful mottled-red blushes of embarrassment. That is, if she could recognize a flirtatious or seductive innuendo when it was tossed at her. He doubted she knew the difference, which was just as well. God help him if she *had* been inclined to dalliance.

In his room he struggled to remove his boots, fingerprinting their glossy surface and resolved to have MacDowell with him on his next visit—if there was a next visit.

He had just heaved them both off with one last powerful oath when there was a light tapping on the door.

His heart skittered uncomfortably about in his chest. It wouldn't—she couldn't possibly—

He pulled open the door and to his intense relief the girl who stood there was the pretty young housemaid who earlier had delivered his water. She was so shaken by the giggles that a steaming mug she carried seemed in immediate danger of being dashed to the hardwood floor.

He rescued the mug, which was brimful of an aromatic brew that filled the hall with the smell of cinnamon and fermented apples.

"Who are you, girl, and what is this?" he asked the maid in great good humor, sniffing pleasurably at the mug.

"I'm Polly, sir—and this is—hot mulled cider—Miss Julianne—she always has us— serve it to—the men guests—at night." She punctuated each phrase with a fresh burst of giggles.

"Does hot mulled cider always have this effect on you, Polly? Or is it me?"

"Oh, it was you, sir. I could hear you half-way down the stairs." She rolled her eyes at him. "Those things you said. Especially the last."

He thought of the silent girl in the room next door. If the maid had heard him cursing from such a distance, then the mistress un-doubtedly had too. He bit down hard on his lip, then like Polly, fell to laughing. The hell with Miss Prim-and-Proper. If a few soldiers' oaths were the worst bombardment ever sounded in her ears, she could count herself damn lucky.

He gulped down the steaming cider and handed the empty mug to Polly. "Thank you, girl, it was delicious."

"You should sleep like a baby after that," she told him cheekily and rolled her eyes at him again. "Anything else I can do for you, Major, sir?" She smiled roguishly up at him and gave an amorous little wriggle.

There was no hidden meaning in her words; the approach was blatant. He clapped his hands on her shoulders, turned her about, put his hands on her plump, solid bottom, and gave her a small push in the direction of the stairs.

"Good night, Polly," he dismissed her firmly.

"Good night, Major De Lacey." She grinned back over her shoulder. "I hope you have a good night's sleep, sir, and lovely dreams."

The mulled cider, a comfortable mattress, the soothing scent of the spiced pomander that someone—he suspected, Julianne—had placed beneath his pillow while he played chess combined with overwhelming fatigue to make Polly's coquettish wish come true.

Having stripped off his clothes and thrown them carelessly onto a chair—MacDowell would be far from pleased when he saw their sorry state—too weary to don his nightshirt, he crawled under the covers, fully prepared to toss and turn and torment himself with thoughts of Amalie, as he had so many other nights. Instead he fell instantly asleep.

He awoke not long after dawn with the red sun stinging his eyelids—he had forgotten to close the blinds—and his blankets tangled at the bottom of the bed. Rolling over with a groan, he hid his face in the pillow. After some moments he realized that he not only felt wide-awake but wonderfully rested and energetic. The only thing that really ailed him was a ravenous hunger.

He rose, strode naked across the room to wash, and discovered that the water was hot. A good fairy—he suspected Polly this time—had supplied it while he slept. He grinned as he lathered his face for shaving, thinking of the pulled-down blankets. Young Polly had gotten more of an eyeful than she was expecting. Her own fault, he decided virtuously. She should knock before creeping and crawling about a strange gentleman's bedchamber.

Just the same, in case she was minded to do it again, he got into his small clothes, then finished shaving, washed and dressed with speed. He had a notion Cousin Frederick would object to dalliance with his housemaid, even if *she* was the one to do the seducing.

"Breakfast is not for another hour, sir," the older maid, Mary, informed him as he glanced with some disappointment into the dining room and found it empty. "In the small parlor," she added helpfully.

"I'll take a walk about the grounds then." He eyed her with a look of mingled hope and speculation. "Mary." His smile and caressing voice were the ones that made the housekeeper at Beaumont his devoted and willing slave. "I don't suppose you could spare a crust of bread and a bit of cheese for a starving man, could you? Just to tide me over till breakfast while I take a stroll."

Mary was no more proof against his blandishments than Mrs. Mercy at home.

"I'll see what I can do, sir," she promised and vanished in the direction of the kitchen.

Five minutes later she was back with a red and white checked napkin tied at the corners like a peddler's sack. "There you are, sir. The bread's still warm from the oven and the apple pie's hotted up—Cook was that upset last night when you didn't even try it—and the cheese was just cut from a fresh new wheel."

"Bless you, dear Mary, this will be recorded in your favor on the Day of Judgment." As he accepted the napkin, Alex tried to press a coin into her hand.

She backed away from the coin and it fell onto the faded Oriental carpet.

"No, indeed, sir, thank you very much. I get paid a good wage for doing my work, and it wouldn't be proper to accept money for doing a guest a small kindness."

He stooped to retrieve the coin, which perhaps accounted for his flushed face.

"I didn't mean to—to distress you, Mary. In England, you see," he explained awkwardly, "it's customary . . ."

She relented a little, allowing a small smile to replace the look of affronted dignity on her face. "Oh, that's all right, sir," she reassured him graciously. "Coming from all that way across the ocean, I can see as how you wouldn't know any better about some of our Dutch customs in New York than I do about yours."

He was still staring after her in disbelief when she removed herself in stately fashion from his presence. After wandering across the formal gardens, he passed through a flowering wilderness, then headed toward the river. "By God!" Alex said aloud wonderingly a few minutes afterward, as he munched on the warm bread and melting cheese, "a Beaumont apologizing to a housemaid! But then, a housemaid with the pride of a peeress! What a country! We'll never get the best of them."

Finishing the last of the crusty bread, he brushed the crumbs from his jacket to feed the birds and started in on the apple pie. He had just taken his first appreciative bite into the flaky crust when he heard again the same high sweet childlike soprano presumed to belong to the mysterious Melrosa. This time her voice did not ring out in the melancholy way that it had the night before when she sang as though *London Bridge* were a dirge rather than a children's jolly play song.

She caroled merrily, joyously the ditty used alternately by each army to plague the other.

And there we see a thousand men,
As rich as 'squire David,
And what they wasted every day,
I wish it had been saved.

Yankey doodle keep it up, yankey doodle dandy
Mind the music and the step
And with the girls be handy.

He had been leaning against the broad flat side of a seven-foot-high spire-shaped boulder watching some fishing boats on the river.

When *Yankey Doodle* began, he looked about in every direction for a glimpse of the girl singer. There was none. Curious and intrigued, he reached up to put napkin and pie on top of the rock pile while he conducted a more determined search.

He went fifty yards forward, backtracked, swung first east, then west, but from the moment he moved, the singing stopped and the only tangible results of his exploration were a thorn scratch on one cheek and a tear on the sleeve of his jacket.

Muttering some of the military expletives that had set Polly giggling the night before, he went to retrieve the napkin and his pie before returning to the house.

He stopped six feet short of the boulder. A small girl stood in its tall shadow, a very fairy of a girl with masses of hair, so blond as to be golden, streaming over her shoulders and spilling down her back. He was unable to determine if the single garment she wore was an over-long shift or a too-short nightdress. It was made of transparently thin white lawn and came only to her calves, exposing shapely unstockinged ankles and slender bare begrimed feet. Every appealing curve of firm, young, rounded buttocks showed from the rear and firm, young rounded breasts from in front.

At the sound of his sucked-in breath, she wheeled around to face him, and he saw that, just like a squirrel, she had been using both hands to cram his pie between her pretty red lips.

Full pretty red lips, full pretty red cheeks in the smooth tanned oval of her pretty face. Pretty! Hell, she was as beautiful as Amalie. Except that the sparkling blue eyes seemed suddenly dilated in terror. As he took one step forward, she took two steps back, tossing away what was left of the pie.

"Hey, there!" he said in teasing protest. "That was *my* breakfast."

He took another step towards her, but she continued to retreat, making queer little animal sounds deep in her throat.

"Melrosa. You *are* Melrosa, aren't you?"

She shook her head, not speaking, and pressed clenched fists against her breast, whimpering.

"You mean, you are *not* Melrosa?"

With a panicked wail, she turned to run, tripped over a fallen tree trunk, and fell heavily. As he knelt to help her up, she rolled over and away from him, cowering, her arms crossed over her face.

"Don't hurt me," she panted from behind her hands. "Please don't hurt Melrosa."

"My dear girl, I am only trying to help you up."

"Please move away from her, Cousin."

He whirled at the sound of Frederick's voice.

"If you will move away, Cousin," Frederick said again, "she will be less fearful."

As Alexander stepped back, Frederick got in front of him, his hands stretched down to the girl. The fear faded from her face. With a sudden radiant smile, she accepted the two hands and allowed herself to be pulled onto her feet.

"Uncle." She hopped onto her toes to kiss his cheek, then stood quietly while he brushed the dirt and leaves from her dress.

"It was wrong of you, Melrosa, to have run out without telling Julianne," he chided her gently. "You know how she worries."

Like a child being scolded, she hung her head, lips trembling, her eyes blinking back tears.

"Nay then, no weeping, my little French Rose," he told her in a voice both gruff and tender. "We are not angry with you, neither of us. Julianne is waiting with your breakfast. Would you not like to pick some flowers for her?"

"Oh, yes," she breathed, all smiles as she skipped away.

To the silent watcher she seemed incredibly childlike, though the bouncing breasts told a different story.

"How old is she?" he asked Frederick abruptly.

"Nineteen. No, I lose track of time. Soon she will be twenty."

"Almost twenty! Good God! She looks about twelve. That is, her figure is a young woman's, but she acts like—"

"Will you come with me, Cousin?" Frederick interrupted him.

"Yes, certainly, wherever you wish."

"Melrosa went back toward the house. If we hurry, she will still be outside."

They both walked quickly, Alex conscious of an urgency he could not explain. As they crossed a flat wooden bridge across the narrowest end of the duck pond, they could see Melrosa on the other side, a clutch of wildflowers in each of her hands. She was dipping, swaying, and swirling around on the grass in an abandoned, graceful, gypsylike dance, her golden hair, sun-red now, fluttering behind her like a banner.

Alex gripped the bridge rail, holding his breath. By God, but there was something sensual in the very innocence of that barefoot dance, in the flimsy bit of cotton that barely offered her decent cover.

Hardly aware of what he was doing, he started moving towards her, but Frederick put a hand on his arm. "No, let her go ahead of us. I don't want her frightened again."

"Is she so afraid of every stranger?"

"No, Cousin, only those who wear uniforms."

"Uniforms?"

"Hessian uniforms. Or British."

Chapter Ten

Lacey Manor, Summer 1779

Melrosa: Latin through the Greek, "honey of roses."
In medieval French legend, she was a fairy.

—*A Book of Names*

WHEN BREAKFAST WAS OVER, JULIANNE EX-
cused herself to attend to household duties; a
number of officers were expected for luncheon, she explained.

The Major gladly accepted Frederick's invitation to walk toward the deer park, wanting
to be alone with his cousin.

"About Melrosa," he began as soon as this
ambition was accomplished. "Her strange-
ness—her fears; you implied they were caused
by the sight of my—a uniform."

"Your pardon, Cousin, I did not imply, I stated it in plain terms. As nearly as we can piece out her story, she was ravished by three soldiers, two of them Hessians, one British, possibly an officer."

Alex bit back his initial impulse to protest. No use pretending such things did not happen, and that officers were not sometimes as guilty as the common soldier. He cleared his throat. "She must have been very young."

"Scarce seventeen. A very sweet and innocent seventeen. She was the youngest of Jacob's daughters and the one he favored most for her resemblance to her dead mother—not so much in coloring, Solange Melrose was exotically dark—but in her sparkle and vivacity. He spoiled her a little, perhaps, but not outrageously so, only enough to keep rough winds from her so that she had no defense against the cruel reality of soldiers at war.

"Never shall I forget the first time I saw her after it had happened." Frederick's eyes took on a wintery chill, his voice grew harsh in remembrance. "They killed her father first, you know. It was during the first fire, the great one in '76 that all but destroyed lower New York. They tossed Jacob alive into the blazing bonfire that was his house. She watched them do it before they turned on her. Nothing in her life had prepared her for men become savage beasts—except that the most ferocious beasts in the animal kingdom do not rape the female of their species as man does."

"I do not know what to say, sir." Alex was sweating more profusely than in the heat and stress of the battle on Long Island. He could see her dancing barefoot on the grass, hear the sweet childlike voice singing *London Bridge*. He looked down at his uniform, for the first time in his career taking no pride in it. "You make me ashamed, Cousin Frederick."

Frederick laid a comforting hand on the younger man's arm. "That was not my intention, Cousin. You have become so involved with my girls, I just wanted you to understand them better. Even though Amalie and Julianne were both on a visit to Trenton at the time and were not brutalized, they all suffered much the same loss that night—of their father, their home, their fortune, their pride, their faith in God's goodness and their innocent belief that the world was good."

Major Alexander De Lacey of the British Army, by way of compensation—out of respect to his more decorous American cousin—for holding back the oaths that would have somewhat relieved his own feelings, pounded a clenched fist against the huge twisted trunk of an aged oak.

He roared out, "Oh, Christ!" as some splinters of tree bark pierced his knuckles, glancing with some apprehension at Frederick as he plucked the splinters out.

96

Frederick was smiling faintly, and Alex gave him an answering if somewhat sheepish smile, as he wrapped a handkerchief around his bleeding fingers, tucking the end of it in under his palm.

"So, perhaps, in the future," Frederick continued as they resumed their walk, "you may be a little more charitable than most people are that Amalie is deemed a wanton because she acts on the public stage and has taken a protector, Julianne is seemingly become a cold-hearted prude, while Melrosa—poor child —is called a lunatic!"

"In one thing they are fortunate, Cousin Frederick," Alex told him with the utmost sincerity. "They—Melrosa, particularly—have you."

"It is no sacrifice on my part," Frederick said with equal sincerity. "Melrosa is—they are all my joy. Not only was their father my friend, but their mother—ah!" He shook his head, smiling fondly. "I loved her, too, more than Jacob, I used to think, even though it was plain from the start that she had eyes only for him. We both met her at a party the first week she came on a visit to New York from New Rochelle, where her father's family— French Huguenots—had settled a full century before. Her mother's people were Dutch like Jacob's. All the beaux in New York—and she had plenty of beaux, I can tell you, in spite of her family's lack of money—used the literal translation of her name for her, the Honey

Rose. But to Jacob she was ever his French Rose; and after their marriage, when Melrosa was born, they both called her their *petite* French Rose. Ah, God protect her, now they call her a Bedlamite!"

"Will she ever"—Alex hesitated—"I am sure you have had doctors for her. Do they think she will ever be fully recovered?"

"Doctors!" Frederick snorted. "All they know is bleeding and pills and, of course, their payments. She does better with Julianne's garden herbs and our loving care. The doctors look wise, shake their heads, and say, perhaps, but I know for a certainty that she will be completely herself one day. Already, there are long periods when she is as rational as you or I—sometimes for weeks at a time. Then some upset or memory reanimates the terror, as it did last night. Still, deep down there is in Melrosa great strength of will to survive, and it is that strength which will one day rise up in her to conquer all the other feelings. Then she will return to us entirely."

"I pray you may be right, Cousin Frederick," Alex said, unwontedly humble in the face of the other's shining faith.

Frederick took a square of white linen from his breeches pocket, blew his nose forcefully, and said, "Well, well, we have been serious enough for one day; you will enjoy the company that comes to luncheon, I think. A number of the officers participated in the coastal raids on Connecticut last month. Tell me, what think you of Sir Henry's war of attrition. Will it serve?"

"As well as doing nothing, I suppose." Alex shrugged. "I was with Clinton in June when we captured Stony Point and Verplancks Point, and later when we launched the first Connecticut attack. We then stopped all action for lack of the reinforcements he thought necessary, and I was among those sent back to New York."

Sir Henry's strategy—or lack of it—in doing so was the chief topic of discussion at the luncheon table, with Sir Henry's officers equally divided about the feasibility of his tactics, each man hotly arguing his own stand.

Frederick sat at the head of the table, endeavoring to calm the participants when they became too vehement, while Julianne, at the foot, pressed food upon their guests in the occasional pauses, but otherwise sat in indifferent calm and silence, apparently impervious to the storm going on about her.

The gentlemen rode in the afternoon, then sat to cards for an hour before repairing once again to the dining room for a dinner that began in midafternoon and lasted for some three hours as delicious course followed course, each accompanied by its own fine wine, so that the huge crystal monteith bowl in the center of the table was employed again and again to rinse the wineglasses for the next bottle.

After dinner, when the officers again sat down to cards, Julianne curtsied and withdrew, her leaving hardly noticed by anyone except her uncle. Alex had intended to extend her the kindly understanding Frederick had requested, but there was something, he reflected in the quiet of his own room later that night, so repulsive about her cold reserve as to make her eminently forgettable.

Early the next morning he came downstairs wearing, instead of his dress uniform, his plainest breeches, riding boots, and a soft white cotton shirt with ruffles at the throat and wrist.

He let himself out of the house, glad neither Frederick nor Julianne was about, and made directly for the duck pond. He could see her long before he got there. This time her garment was most obviously a nightdress for it was made of a thin but less revealing flannel, buttoned modestly up to her throat and falling below her ankles. Her feet, however, were bare again, and her dance was faster, wilder, more abandoned than the day before, with the long gold hair whirling in the air like a battle pennant and the constant twisting movements of her hands and arms so sensual that the responsive tightening of his throat was accompanied by a shaming tightening of his breeches.

With a strong effort he subdued all feeling except the one that had brought him creeping downstairs in the early dawn. Slowly and steadily he walked towards her, and when he came as near as he thought wise, he stood silent and still under the shade of a young white elm, one hand stretched up to grip the lowest branch on which was slung a basket heaped with roses. Hers, no doubt.

Presently the circling of her dance brought her near enough to see him, and she gave a little cry of fear as she stopped dead.

For several minutes they stood there, both motionless, Melrosa frozen with fear, Alex deliberately not making the slightest sound or movement, not so much as the blink of an eye that might further alarm her.

When he did close his eyes for some seconds to shut out the sight of her, unfortunately, the heady scent of her roses, the dewy grass, and the sweet fresh morning air together with the picture in his mind's eye proved as powerful an aphrodisiac as her dance.

He opened his eyes and found her almost upon him, moving stealthily, one arm upraised to recover her basket. As soon as she saw him watching, she gave another little cry and started backing off again.

He released the basket from the branch and set it on the ground, then backed away himself. From a distance of ten feet, he invited softly, "Come get your flowers, child; I won't prevent you."

She hesitated, and he sat down on the grass, knees raised, hands clasped about them.

"Take your basket, Melrosa," he told her in a

voice of gentle persuasion, his eyes never leaving her face.

Like one mesmerized, she moved forward, slowly at first, and then with the speed of a frightened deer, snatching at the basket and once more leaping back.

He thought she might dart off again and felt a surge of triumph when she hesitated and turned around, standing at a safe distance but nevertheless staying.

"You dance beautifully, Melrosa. I like to watch you."

She bit down on the knuckles of her left hand, eyeing him warily. Then from the recesses of her mind, she dredged up some dim-remembered lesson of courtesy, bobbed a child's curtsey, and whispered to him, "Thank you, sir."

There was a pause.

"It's a lovely day," he ventured after a while.

She considered this seriously, looked all about, then smiled in sudden beauty. "Lovely," she agreed with a vigorous shake of her head.

"I like to sit on the grass on a lovely day," he offered next, patting the grass near to him as though it were a puppy.

"Melrosa, too," she said happily. "*I* like to sit on the grass." A note of doubt crept into her voice. "Nurse said proper little ladies don't."

"You're not a *little* lady any more." He patted the grass again.

She drew a few hesitant steps near to him, and his heart thumped hard and triumphantly.

"I sat on the grass once and got stains on my white Sunday muslin," she told him, like a child offering a confidence. Her tone became slightly aggrieved, and she put one hand behind her, rubbing her bottom. "Nurse spanked me."

He smothered a smile.

"You are too old to spank," he told her gravely. "You're all grown up now. Look at me. *I'm* grown up, and I'm sitting on the grass."

She treated him once more to that sudden radiant smile, then plumped herself down on the grass, still cautious enough not to sit quite close.

"You won't hurt me?" she asked him.

His chest tightened painfully. "I promise I will never hurt you, Melrosa," he said quietly.

"You are a nice man," she pronounced, setting the basket onto her lap. "I think—yes, you may be my friend."

"Thank you, Melrosa. I doubt if I have ever had a compliment that meant more to me."

In a sudden access of shyness, she buried her face in her roses but presently looked up to smile sweetly across at him. She seemed to read something in his return smile that struck a chord deep within her. Across the few feet of space that separated them, she extended a trembling hand to him.

It lay in his like a frightened bird at first, and then with gathering confidence tightened around his fingers, gripping and clinging.

Frederick, coming across the lawn a little later, heard her voice first.

Yankey doodle keep it up, yankey doodle dandy,
Mind the music and the step
And with the girls be handy.

Then he stopped, staring in astonishment at the two sitting side by side, their hands clasped together.

Melrosa saw him first. She sprang up joyfully, calling out his name. Then she pointed down to Alexander. "This nice man is my friend."

Frederick said huskily, doubtfully, "Melrosa?"

She flung her arms around his neck. "I love you, Uncle Frederick," she declared extravagantly. "Now I will return to Julianne."

She bent for her basket, flashed one more smile at Alex and ran off, calling back to him, "Good-bye, new friend."

"Au revoir, Melrosa," he said so softly that only Frederick heard him.

Alex got to his feet. He had expected Frederick to be overjoyed. Instead he seemed strangely disturbed.

"Is something wrong, Cousin Frederick? I thought it was a good sign that I could coax her to sit with me and talk, even to touch my hand. It inclines me to believe you were right in what you said. Someday she will be fully recovered."

"She is still—in spite of what happened to her—such an innocent. God help her if—"

"My God!" Alex paled as he suddenly understood the other's troubled face. "What kind of oversexed monster do you think me? I am no saint, Cousin, but neither am I a rapist or a seducer of disturbed children. My women are both willing and aware. Melrosa—any man might desire her loveliness—but only one lost in degeneracy would take advantage of her condition. She is springtime, she is joy. She is a fairy beauty. And, in the sense you mean, she is untouchable."

"Forgive me," said Frederick. "She is all I have, and I would protect her with my life. I am the only sure protection *she* has."

"Your concern for her is only natural," Alex forced himself to say. "I think I do understand."

As he looked at the older man's suddenly ravaged face, he felt a wrench of pity, understanding more, far more than the guardian double her age might have wished him to.

Chapter Eleven

New York, Autumn 1779

Last stanza† of "Cow Chase," a Satiric Poem by Major John André, published serially in Rivington's *Gazette*.

> And now I've closed my epic strain
> I tremble as I show it,
> Lest this same warrior-drover, Wayne,*
> Should ever catch the poet.

†The last stanza appeared on Sept. 23, 1780, the day of André's capture.
*Major General Anthony Wayne was the American officer in whose custody André was placed while awaiting trial.

THE MAJOR'S VISIT TO HIS NEWFOUND COUSIN lasted another five days, during which there were constant comings and goings of fellow officers, some of them already staying at Sir

Henry's neighboring property, others riding all the way from their posts to the north or south or at headquarters in the city, all for the sake of tasting the famed hospitality of the loyalist Frederick De Lacey's Turtle Bay estate.

During those days Alex saw Melrosa twice more, the first time dancing near the duck pond as she had before, the second on the dock that extended out in the bay. She was giggling girlishly as she tossed flowers from her basket to the eager, laughing men in the fishing boats below.

The first time she saw him she was willing to sit with him on the grass as she had before, but at their next encounter, when he approached her, she ran away. He did not follow after her, and his reward for his forbearance was a flashing smile when she reached the front lawn and turned to look in his direction. Then she waved her hand and whisked around to the back of the house.

On the day he was to return to New York, breakfast was served early, and afterward he took a last walk around the grounds in Frederick's company. When he went up to his room to pack his portmanteau, he found Julianne there ahead of him and his packing almost completed.

She looked up at his little exclamation of surprise, flushing slightly.

"It was nothing," she said in reply to his

courteous protest. "I have never yet known a man who could pack properly."

He smiled slightly. "So far as I am concerned, my batman MacDowell would agree with you; he deems me incapable in matters of my own care. He would, though, hotly dispute what you said as regards himself, whom he considers more efficient than any woman."

Julianne smiled back, a tight prim smile but nevertheless the first time he could remember her ever doing so. "Then you must bring him with you the next time you visit," she said agreeably. "In the meantime, Major, it was my pleasure. I—I—"

She stole a quick nervous look at him from under long lashes.

"Cousin Alex, I—I—"

"Yes, Cousin Julianne?"

She clasped her two hands against her breast, her fingers knotted together.

"I know I have not always been as—as—Uncle Frederick reproached me that I am sometimes lacking in—in courtesy to you, but I—but I—"

He strode forward and took her by the shoulders, at which her face broke out in violent blushes.

"Why don't you just spit it out, Cousin?" he invited her somewhat crudely. "All this simpering and blushing does not seem quite your style."

"Oh!" She pushed him away indignantly. "You are the most infuriating man!"

He grinned. "That's more like you, Cousin Julianne. I knew such extraordinary civility could not last long."

"Well, you are mistaken!" she retorted with energy. "In spite of your own lack of courtesy, I nevertheless wish to apologize for any lack there may have been in *my* manners to you this past week."

His grin widened, and he clapped lightly, as at a theater performance. "Well done, Cousin. It takes rare talent to render an apology so that the recipient feels he is guilty of some wrong."

Her face settled into its usual humorless mask. "Is that what I did? Oh, dear!" She was all but wringing her hands. "I can't do anything right. Truly, I did mean to express my most heartfelt regret for having misjudged you and not always—",

He came forward and once more took her by the shoulders. "Gently, gently," he said. "I was but teasing. Pray how have you misjudged me?"

"You are a soldier," she whispered, head bent.

"Ah. You are prejudiced against British soldiers because of Melrosa?"

Her head lifted as she once more removed herself from his grasp. A not-unbecoming flush diminished the sallowness of her complexion. "Not just British soldiers," she said defiantly. "*Any* soldiers. British or American, there is nothing to choose between you."

"So, like Amalie, you are a neutral?"

"No, not at all like Amalie," she spat at him. "Her so-called neutrality is of the sort that makes her deal quite willingly with any of you so long as it profits her. Mine is the opposite kind. British or American, you both leave a trail of death and destruction in your wake wherever you go. I say, a plague on both your houses!"

"I see," said Alex. "A most comprehensive apology, Cousin Julianne."

Once more her face looked stricken.

"I really meant it to be," she muttered. "I am not unmindful of how kind you have been, how great a debt I—we owe you, and—"

"Kind? A debt? What on earth are you talking about?"

She stood up straight, shoulders braced, speaking this time with quiet dignity. "Kind to Melrosa," she said. "You may perhaps not realize, having never seen her before this week, but you have helped her immeasurably. She has made greater strides in recovery since you have been here than—oh, in many months that have gone before."

"I think you do me too much credit," he said gently. "Nothing could ever match the tireless and devoted care that I have seen you give her. Still, if I have contributed in any way to her recovery, that fact is reward enough. She is a lovely child, a—a—"

"A honey rose?"

"Exactly."

She took an impulsive step toward him. "But I do feel grateful, and you must allow me to tell you so."

"I accept your apology and your thanks. Now," he told her quite firmly, "the subject is closed." He slung his portmanteau from the bed onto the floor. "Do you think—would it be possible for me to say good-bye to Melrosa?"

She said slowly, after a moment's serious reflection, "I think perhaps it would be better not. We have found that it unsettles her to say good-bye to the few people for whom she feels any attachment; she seems to have this fear of abandonment by those she loves. She is a little vague about time, so if she does not see you, she may think you are likely to be somewhere else about the place. You will be returning soon for another visit"—her voice was almost pleading—"will you not?"

"The moment my duties allow," he pledged and saw for the first time, in her brilliant flashing smile, a strong resemblance to her two beautiful sisters.

There was even a gleam of humor too. "Be sure to bring your MacDowell, too," she told him over her shoulder as she scooted out the door.

A little later she stood beside Frederick on

the portico where they said their good-byes, and after he had shaken Frederick's hand, she allowed her own to be kissed without any undue fuss and only the slightest heightening of color.

As his horse reached the end of the graveled driveway and trotted through the swinging wood gates, he heard a sad little voice singing somewhere far off:

> *London Bridge is falling down*
> *Falling down*
> *Falling down*

He reined in his horse and called out softly several times, "Melrosa!" When there was no answer, just the whisper of the trees, the cries of birds, and the bleat of a solitary sheep wandered off from the herd, he called much more loudly, "Melrosa!" Then, "I will be back," he shouted out. "I promise you, Melrosa, I will be back."

New York was much as he had left it, with soldiers and civilians alike wilting in the humid heat and most social activity stopped.

The theater was still closed, but André had returned from another of his mysterious journeys and spent most of his days engaged with a voluminous correspondence and in the composition of secret memorandums.

Alex De Lacey, who knew him as few others among their fellow officers did and was one of the few not jealous of his uncommonly rapid rise in rank as well as in Sir Henry Clinton's trust and affection, sensed the excited jubilance beneath his outwardly calm manner.

"Something is brewing, and you know of it," he challenged his friend one afternoon as they sat together in Rivington's Coffeehouse.

André smiled wisely and provokingly, his only answer a languid, protesting wave of one white hand.

"Save that affected sort of flummery for someone who doesn't know you better," Alex told him caustically.

André laughed out loud. "My information, Alexander, is this—Lord Cornwallis' return to America has caused Sir Henry once again to beg the King's permission to retire."

"Tired news, my friend. Everyone at Staff is aware of this latest resignation and that Clinton is displaying characteristic petulance over Cornwallis' so-called 'dormant commission,' which is only a common-sense insurance that the succession never falls to a higher-ranking Hessian."

"This should not be generally spoken of, but *entre nous,* the plans for the southern campaign have been reanimated."

"*Entre nous!*" Alex scoffed. "Come now, John. *That* is the most ill-kept secret on Manhattan isle."

"It is quite definite now. Say nothing, but we will leave before the winter."

"I will say nothing," Alex said, "but pray

113

you see what you can do for me, John. I want—nay, I intend to be part of this next expedition. I have spent enough of this war that Clinton conducts so strangely hanging about New York wearing a shine on the bottom of my breeches. Do you go too?"

"Yes, as Deputy Adjutant, and I will present your request to Sir Henry—much more tactfully worded."

Alex laughed, but when he and André were walking along the cobbled streets again, he studied him shrewdly.

"Do you think you have fooled me, my friend, just because I allowed myself to be diverted? It is not Sir Henry's latest resignation or the prospect of the southern campaign —though I know you have urged it strenuously—that has you in such a state of inner ferment."

"I must be getting obvious." André laughed. "In my profession," he quipped, "one should not be obvious."

"Soldiering is not exactly a subtle business," Alex reminded him. "Why should you be different than any of the rest of us?"

There was a short pause before André said, with a slight smile, "You are correct. Why should I be different than any other soldier?" Then he added more seriously, "It is true there is something brewing, something that could be of immeasurable value to our side. It is equally important that it not be talked of, not even speculated on. Can I count on you for that, De Lacey?"

"Always," Alex answered. "The matter is hereby laid to rest." Gracefully, he turned the subject. "Just how do you plan to word *your* tactful request for *my* active duty in the southern campaign?" he asked earnestly.

They passed the rest of their walk with many a jest as to how Sir Henry's compliance could be won, but jest or not, only a fortnight later, Clinton's positive consent was given.

Immediately, not knowing just how soon they would depart the garrison at New York, De Lacey applied for leave so he could once again go to Turtle Bay. In case the departure of the troops was speeded up, he wanted to be able first to pay a visit to his cousin.

He was quite willing to admit to himself that he was even more concerned to keep his promise to Melrosa. He had sworn to her that he would return, and he did not intend to fail her.

As it turned out, Headquarters was as dilatory about the start of the southern campaign as about most other operations. Delay followed delay, so that De Lacey was able to pay not one but three visits to Lacey Manor before he departed New York.

He went there in late September, during early November, and in mid-December, taking MacDowell with him. His batman, to De Lacey's amused respect, having carefully donned a fringed buckskin hunting shirt and workmens' breeches borrowed from one of Frederick's farmers in place of his frightening red uniform, went prowling around the grounds day after day till he found Melrosa and won her over completely.

She returned to the house during their November visit actually skipping alongside MacDowell, and before she went up to her room gravely presented the batman with a spray of wildflowers from her basket and bade him a quiet good-bye. "What did you say? What did you do?" Frederick demanded of the corporal.

"Yon lassie needs to be spoken to just like any other girl," MacDowell pronounced sagely. "It's this business of treating her like an invalid that does all the harm. She is no' an invalid, and 'tis foolishness—he glared at Frederick—to turn her into one, acting as though she's made out of glass instead of the fine sturdy lassie she is."

He stumped off into the house, leaving Frederick amused rather than annoyed. He waved away Alex's attempt at apology. "Your man is an original; he should stay in America, Cousin, where such quality is more appreciated."

"I would miss him if he did," Alex grinned. "He adds spice to what is mostly a cursed dull life."

"Your life in New York is dull with the theater open again and all the dining and drinking and dancing that goes on among the officers?"

"I see you have your spies, Cousin Frederick." Alex's smile was strained. "The truth is," he said after a moment's hesitation, "that Amalie has not yet returned from Jersey and life in New York—with her gone—is indeed most damnably dull!"

"You seem content when you are here at Lacey Manor," Frederick murmured.

"That is different. Lacey Manor is not New York. Here I have your company . . . and then there is Melrosa."

"Yes, to be sure, Melrosa."

"I have come to have as great an interest in her welfare as I would if she were my sister," Alex explained earnestly.

"I am sure she thinks of you like a brother," said Frederick quietly.

The next day Julianne had the kitchen pack a basket full of food for a picnic for her sister and the Major. Melrosa came down from her third-floor room, properly dressed for the first time since he had met her in a pair of sturdy shoes, a gown and a cloak, with her golden hair bundled beneath a bonnet.

Alex and she walked hand-in-hand to the river, where they talked and laughed, ate heartily, exchanged occasional happy glances of silent understanding. She sang for him, this time only joyful songs. Then, after lunch she sat snuggled up to him and, childlike, put her head on his shoulder and dozed off.

Before he left for New York the next day, she asked him, her eyes wide and imploring, "Promise me you will come again soon."

"I promise," he said, the image of her so strongly in his heart and mind it seemed an easy vow to keep—until late November when Amalie came home to New York.

Chapter Twelve

I know not, I ask not, if guilt's in that heart,
I but know that I love thee whatever thou art.

—*Thos. Moore*

FOLLOWING A CONVIVIAL FEW HOURS WITH
some fellow-officers at Rivington's Coffeehouse, Alex parted company with his friends
and walked over to Rivington's print shop to
pick up the first American editions of Sheridan's plays, newly printed by the publisher.
When he left on the southern campaign, they
would make an admirable parting gift for his
landlady, Mrs. Phelps, who had a passion for
the theater.

Rivington was at the back of his store, talking earnestly to a lady in a cloak of dark blue wool, its hood thrown over her head. He smiled recognition at the Major, who sketched a slight courteous gesture with one hand to indicate that he would wait. The lady's hood fell back against her shoulders, revealing a familiar powdered head on a slender neck with the carriage of a queen.

"Amalie!" he said in a husky whisper but not so low that she did not hear him.

She half-turned, her color rising and inclined her head towards him, making a formal half-curtsey.

"Amalie!" he said again, springing forward.

"Major."

"I did not know—no one told me—your name was on no theater bill—"

Rivington turned his head to conceal his smiles at this jumble of incoherencies while Amalie said with the utmost composure, "I only returned to town two days ago. I will not perform until the end of next week, and there has been no time at my disposal to contact my *friends*."

Her slight emphasis was not lost on Alex nor her cold shoulder as she turned back to Rivington. "I would be obliged, sir, if you would send word to the theater when my order is ready."

"With the greatest pleasure, Madame Nostrand."

"Good day, gentlemen."

"Your servant, ma'am," said Rivington, but

Alex followed her out of the shop, by no means willing to accept this dismissal.

"Will you have dinner with me tonight, Amalie?"

"No, Major, I will not."

"Tomorrow?"

"Not tomorrow, Major. Not ever."

"Why?" he asked baldly.

"Why?" she repeated bitterly. "*You* have the audacity to ask me that. Your memory must be very short, Major, or extremely convenient. Recollect, our friendship was ended by *your* desire. You said you wanted no part of me if I went to Trenton. Well, I went." She tossed the elegant head of powdered hair, loosening a spray of flowers that fastened above some side curls. "And whenever I so desire—or *he* does—I shall go again." Her laughter was both brittle and mocking. "Do you still wish to have dinner with me, sir?"

He seized her by her cloaked shoulders, looking down into the proud, defiant, and bewitchingly lovely face.

"Yes, damn it!" He ground out the words. "I still want to have dinner with you."

She blinked several times in surprise; then suddenly and surprisingly the brilliant blue eyes were awash in tears. She uttered the same, single one-word question that he had, only hers came out in a stammered whisper, "W-wh-why?"

"Don't play games with me, Amalie. I may be leaving New York soon, and I don't want to waste the little time we may have left. You know damned well that I am mad for you, but if friendship is all that you have to give me, then I will accept even that half-loaf."

"Leaving New York!" she exclaimed in fright. "For the fighting in the South? Is all the headquarters staff going with Sir Henry instead of staying on in New York?"

"What do you know of the fighting in the South?"

"Oh, my dear." She clasped both hands around his arm, fresh tears trembling on her lashes. "All of New York knows that Clinton's departure with a good part of the New York garrison only awaited the news of the enemy French fleet off the Southern coast." Her hands moved up and down his sleeve in unconscious caress. "I thought because you were a staff officer, you might"—she looked up at him, biting down on her lower lip, then completed the shamed confession—"I thought you might stay safely here in New York."

"I am a soldier, Amalie."

"I know." She lowered her head for a moment so he could not see her face. "When do you go?"

"I am not sure. Days. A few weeks. Does it matter?"

She lifted her head to meet his hungry gaze, staring up at him, prideful and arrogant again, as well as dry-eyed. "I wondered how much time we might have left to spend together," she told him shamelessly.

"Amalie, oh, Amalie."

His arms slipped under the cloak to bring her into a breathless, bone-breaking embrace. There on the open streets of New York, with passing ladies to sniff disdainfully and harlots to make lewd comments, loiterers to cheer and little boys to hoot, they shared their first long, loving kiss.

After some time, still under the eyes of the interested, the merging mouths separated slightly. "Seven o'clock for dinner?" he murmured.

She pressed quivering fingers to her equally-quivering lips. "S-s-seven o'clock," she agreed, in something of a daze.

All their free evenings during the next week were spent together in public dining, public dancing, or attending concerts or other public performances at the theater. For the following Sunday afternoon he proposed a country drive and luncheon at an inn.

The moment they were closed inside, with the driver on his seat and the closed carriage in motion, he seized her in his arms.

"By God!" he said with feeling. "What I have to resort to in order to get you alone!"

"Alone—at an inn?" Her mouth primmed even as her eyes laughed at him.

"Oh, I forgot to tell you. There has been a

slight change in plans." He set her back on the cushions, lifted a basket from the floor of the coach and wedged it between them. "Luncheon is served—right here."

"A carriage picnic," she said demurely as he spread a linen cloth across her lap. "A new conceit of the aristocracy, perhaps?"

"Not at all," he retorted, poking about in the basket. "Military strategy *and* a soldier's desperation. What have we—ah, good, fried chicken. May I help you to a leg?"

"Thank you." She took it gingerly between her fingers.

"And I"—His hands had untied the strings of her cloak and were now dealing deftly with the lacing of her bodice—"I will just nibble on a breast."

"Alexander!"

"Chicken, of course," he said innocently, letting go of her and delving into the basket once again.

Across the thigh bone on which she had been daintily munching, she watched in a kind of horrified fascination as his teeth, strong and white and sharp, slashed down with gusto on a plump chicken breast, reducing it in short order to meatless bones, which he tossed into the basket, wiping his hands carefully on another linen cloth.

She was still staring at him, wide-eyed, her chicken leg arrested in midair, when he chanced to look at her again. Immediately her face was overspread by a violent blush. He cocked his head to one side, and what began as a slow smile turned into a hearty laugh. The more vivid her blushes, the harder he laughed.

"My dear Amalie," he choked out finally between his roars of laughter, "I assure you, the chicken felt no pain." As he spoke, his hands were at her bodice again. "I promise you, I would deal much more gently with *you*."

She pushed his hands away. "I don't know what you are talking about," she told him haughtily, "but I wish you would desist!"

"Desist talking, my little hypocrite, or desist doing?"

"Both, and I am not a hypocrite."

"Well, let us just say," he soothed her, "that your lips are telling me one thing and—er—other parts of your body quite another."

Tears of mortification stood in her eyes. She could not deny what he had discovered for himself, that where his two hands had dipped inside her bodice to curve casually beneath her breasts, there had been an instant reaction. Her breasts, of their own volition, seemed to lift and swell and fill his hands, with the nipples pressing in taut eagerness against his caressing thumbs.

"My darling girl!" He took her by the shoulders, trying to look into her averted face. "I was only teasing. What are you so ashamed of? Amalie." He shook her slightly. "Stop playing the simpering virgin. It is not your role any more than mine is that of the practiced seducer attempting to have his way with you"—he smiled whimsically, inviting her to join him—"in a closed carriage."

"No, my dear." He let go of her and sat back in his own corner. "I am quite determined that if, in the future you should want me, *you* will have to do the asking. You know, you don't really seem too interested in that chicken leg." He gently removed it from her paralyzed grasp. "Would you prefer some cheese and bread, and shall I open the wine?"

"I am not hungry," she told him breathlessly. "But I"—wetting her lips—"yes, I would like a little wine."

He lifted two objects like swaddled dolls from the basket and carefully unwrapped the red and white checked towels from around two delicate crystal wineglasses, holding them up triumphantly to show her. "Unbroken. Hold them, my sweet, while I open the bottle."

When this was accomplished with a minimum of spillage, he poured a half-glass for each of them and continued to pour half-glasses until the bottle was finished.

Their drinking was finished in virtual silence, so it was not till she raised her last half-glass to him, slopping a little of the wine over the rim and down the front of her dress, that he realized she had been more than slightly affected.

"You kn-know why I w-will not—sh-shall

not b-bed w-with you, not ever, Major Alexander De Lacey, s-s-son of the Earl of B-Beaumont?" she hiccuped.

"Good Lord!" he said, steadying her waving hand. Then, with a slightly rueful smile, "No, tell me, Madame Nostrand, why won't you?"

"P-powerful f-feeling betwixt us, we b-both know that."

"We most certainly do."

"But we want different things of—of one 'nother."

"Do we really, Amalie Nostrand?" he whispered, his face very close to hers.

She finished the last of her wine and patted his cheek with the cold edge of the empty glass. "So, so different," she said wistfully. "Our ideas are as far apart"—she flung out her arms to show the vast distance—"as the miles between London and New York. You just want my body, p-poor man." She looked almost sad for him. "And I want my h-heart m-mended."

"Why does your heart need mending, Amalie?"

"C-can't tell you. Can only tell my—my—t-tell someone sp-special. That's why we never can be truly together. You want a mistress, I w-want a true love."

"Was your husband a true love, Amalie? Not the way I heard it."

She blinked owlishly at the sudden ugly edge to his voice.

"My husband is dead."

"Why did you marry him, Amalie? Why did you take him away from Julianne?"

These seemed to be sobering questions. When she answered, she seemed almost herself again. "I could say that I wanted him and Julianne did not."

Hearing his snort of disdain, she shrugged. "I was more like you in those days. He had something to offer that I needed, so I grabbed at him quite selfishly, without regard to his need or Julianne's. A bad mistake. I shan't make it twice, for which you"—her smile mocked both him and herself—"should be quite grateful to me."

"I may be as selfish and as grasping as you are—I have no means of measurement—but if you dare to speak again of the gratitude I should feel for your refusal, expect to have your ears soundly boxed," he advised her savagely. "Even if you don't say another word, I may find it impossible to control the urge to do so!"

Slow tears splashed into the empty wineglass clasped against her still-unlaced bodice. She spoke in a series of breathless, disjointed phrases. "My head . . . beginning to ache . . . the wine . . . Tonight . . . must sleep . . . there is early rehearsal called tomorrow . . . If you please, the carriage . . . Turn . . . I must . . . I must go home."

She laid the wineglass on the seat beside her and pulled her cloak about her while he rapped on the window to attract the driver's attention and curtly give the command to drive back toward lower Manhattan.

"Will you have dinner with me tomorrow night?" he asked her presently, as abrupt with the invitation as he had been with the driver.

"It might perhaps be best if we were apart from each other for—for a few days," she suggested, paining both of them.

"Very well then. In that case I shall take the opportunity while we *stay apart*"—his voice was icy with sarcasm—"to go to Lacey Manor. I would like to make my farewells to Cousin Frederick in person. And I gave my word to Melrosa that I would not go away without seeing her again."

"I see."

"I wonder if you do," he murmured and reached over for her hand, which lay limply in his.

His rage seemed to have cooled as suddenly as it had come on him, but her own misery was like a stone lodged in her breast.

"Of course," he suggested after a while, chafing her hand to warm it, "you could come with me to Lacey Manor."

"I? Go to Lacey Manor? You know very well that I cannot."

"Your uncle would welcome you with open arms, and Melrosa would go wild with joy. She has spoken of you to me most lovingly."

"And Julianne, has she spoken of me lovingly, too, or—most likely—not at all?"

She turned to face him, and the pain in her

129

eyes was so great, he yearned to take her in his arms to offer the comfort she would have denied wanting.

"You don't have to say it, I know," she told him dully. "To Julianne, I might as well be dead, and until she numbers me among the living and *asks* me, nay, urges me to come to her, I will never go again to Lacey Manor."

Chapter Thirteen

Turtle Bay, New York,
September, 1780

My true love hath my heart,
And I have his.

—*Sir Philip Sidney*

ON A CRISP COOL SEPTEMBER DAY IN 1780 Major Alexander De Lacey rode through the high wooden gates that gave entrance to Lacey Manor. He took deep thankful gulps of the tangy fresh country air so different from the smoke-choked, fishy, sewage-reeking smells of the city, finding it hard to believe a full ten months had gone by since his last hurried farewell visit.

Frederick De Lacey came down the steps of the house to welcome him, as he had the first time they met, only this time his greeting was to a well-loved kinsman.

"My dear Alex, I received the news of your safety that you so kindly sent after the fall of Charleston in May, but to have you here in the flesh—" He embraced the younger man warmly, stepped back to survey him from head to foot, then removed his spectacles momentarily to wipe his eyes.

Arms linked, they walked into the house.

"Melrosa wept with relief when your letter came, and for the first time in years I heard Julianne sing about the house."

"And Amalie went as usual to Trenton."

"My dear Alex—" There was a note of reprimand mixed with affection in Frederick's voice. "Amalie is, as always, a law unto herself. Because she chooses to hide her deepest feelings does not mean that she has none."

"It is hardly my right to judge the merry widow," said Alex lightly, though in truth, on his return to New York from Charleston, he had passed a very harsh judgment on finding the lady in Jersey instead of in waiting.

"Nor to cast the first stone," Frederick suggested somewhat sternly.

So Frederick knew from Amalie that her only proposal from him had not been one of marriage. What his cousin did *not* know, however, was that, whether for good or ill, war works powerfully on men's emotions.

During the fighting his loved family in England had somehow seemed quite remote to him as well as very far away. His best friends were the soldiers who fought alongside him, his cocky batman who, at Monck's Corner, had taken a bullet in the arm that might otherwise have lodged in his master's chest.

His fondest memories in the din and turmoil and blood of battle had strangely not been of Beaumont but of Lacey Manor. Melrosa dancing near the duckpond in a clinging white shift with a clutch of wildflowers in each of her hands . . . Julianne in her Quaker gown, smelling of fresh-baked bread and smiling a rare sweet smile when she thanked him for his goodness to her sister.

He had thought of Frederick, his clay pipe always clamped between his lips, as he appeased a group of angry officers arguing the conduct of the war or uttered "Checkmate" in a quiet, prosaic manner, the while his eyes twinkled in triumph across a chessboard.

But most of all Amalie . . . Amalie! Amalie of the beautiful, bewitching face and entrancing figure; Amalie, who walked like a queen across a restaurant and brought a whole theater to its feet cheering when she came out on a stage. Amalie, who had stolen her sister's man and then turned wanton barely before the earth settled on his burial mound.

Amalie, who had claimed to want a true love and then not troubled to wait through the fighting to find out that her true love had come safely through and was coming back to tell her he was hers. Hers forever—in any way she wanted.

Major Alexander De Lacey opened his mouth to tell Frederick that he was being misjudged, then closed it again. In view of the past, present self-righteousness would be out of place. Whatever Frederick now thought, he, Alex, had given him reason to think, so he could hardly speak to him about a proposal that had not yet taken place. Time enough for that when Amalie returned. Then he or she, perhaps both together—his mind dwelled pleasurably on that alternative—would do the telling.

Perhaps if Julianne could be brought around, they would be married at Lacey Manor. His mind, as they entered the house, played with delightful pictures. He would like to be married on such a day as this, with Frederick to give the bride away and Melrosa and Julianne as bridesmaids, if the one were well enough and the other could be coaxed into a pretty gown instead of her ugly grays.

"Where is Melrosa? And Cousin Julianne?"

"I know you will be disappointed, Alex, but they are away on a visit. I only had your letter yesterday morning, and by an unlucky chance, they had left the day before for Trenton."

"Trenton?"

"To visit their aunts," Alex repeated in a sudden cold fury. "I see."

"I don't think you do, Cousin."

"And is Amalie also visiting her aunts? I thought she and Julianne were unwilling to stay under the same roof."

"It's unfortunately true that they have not reconciled yet, but Amalie has many friends in the town."

"Friends and lovers, don't you mean?" Alex asked him bitterly.

"No, Cousin, I do not, and neither is it a question I will have asked or answered in my home."

"Good God, Cousin Frederick, I am not just being vulgarly curious!" Alex burst out passionately. "I mean—I meant to marry Amalie when I came back from the South."

"I collect that you mean you intended to ask her if *she* would marry *you*," said Frederick dryly. "Or are you so positive that she is a piece of ripe fruit, ready to fall into your waiting hands at a single slight shake of the tree?"

Alex's slight flush of shame died away. "Yes, I meant to ask her," he said in a more subdued manner.

"And now you no longer do? Because she went to Trenton?"

"I don't know. I will have to wait until I see her."

"That should not be too long. In her last letter she seemed quite certain that she would be in New York no later than this month's end. In fact, I had some thoughts of wintering in Manhattan this year myself if I can per-

suade Sir Henry"—he laughed pleasantly—
"to give me back a small portion of my
house."

"I had no notion that you owned a house in
New York."

"Yes, indeed, a fine mansion my father
built. It is a stone's throw from your headquarters at the Kennedy place. After the fire
in '76, with the great housing shortage, General Howe had more need of it than I so I put it
at the disposal of the army. There was no
generosity involved. I had already resolved to
stay on here with Melrosa until she recovered,
and the doctors had said we must on no
account send her back to the place which—
where her memories would be so painful."

"Would she be willing to stay in Manhattan
with you now? And Julianne as well?"

"I think it might be wise to give it a trial.
They cannot hide here away from the world
forever, and you have no notion"—his face
brightened—"how much better Melrosa is . . .
wait till you see her. She is healthy and glowing; she dresses each day and takes her meals
with us, even sometimes with guests present.
She helps Julianne and the maids about the
house. I have every hope that the time is near
when she will lead an entirely normal life."

"I am sure your hopes are justified, Cousin
Frederick. Why, when I first met her, little
over a year gone by," he reminisced, "she was
a terrified child, creeping around corners,
singing her little dirges. Impossible to think of

her then as you describe her now, traveling abroad, mingling freely with friends and strangers." He sighed a little. "I must confess I am disappointed she is not with you; I long to see all these remarkable changes."

It was true, he thought more than once during the remainder of the day. He missed amazingly the little sister she had become to him, the high sweet voice singing *Yankey Doodle*, the confiding, trusting way her hand would slip into his as they walked together. He even missed Julianne with her mugs of hot mulled cider and her constant cold-water dashes of common sense in mealtime conversation, the calm capability with which she went about her chores, ceaselessly seeing to the care and comfort of the household.

He missed them both in a heart-tugging way that held as much pleasure in recollection as it did pain. But Amalie! He had only to think of her and his guts were wrenched apart. Recollections of Amalie brought only red-hot agony.

He charged about the featherbed like a cavalryman all that night and damned her for what she had done to him. He loved her and he hated her. He was not sure whether he loved or hated more.

He was almost grateful that his visit would be so short; he must return to New York on the morrow. André had left town the week before with the laughing reminder that Sir Henry was now in his charge.

"Take care of him, Alex," had been his last laughing remark, spoken, his friend knew, half in earnest as well as half in jest. Clinton, with his moods and tempers and insecurities, must be carefully nurtured by his staff.

"I cannot promise to be as good a nanny as you," he joked in turn, "but I will do my best."

He had ducked, pretending alarm, as André went into a boxing stance and raised his fists. They were both still laughing when they said farewell.

André might have returned by now; his comings were sometimes as sudden as his goings, but in case not . . . and if Amalie should return before month's end. . . .

Neither was in New York. Clinton, applied to, said with unusual good humor that he had no notion which day his chief aide would return, except that it would be a good day for the British. "A damned good day, Alexander, my boy," he reiterated jubilantly, pounding his hands together with rare enthusiasm.

Ill-humoredly De Lacey attacked the mound of paper work waiting for him, wondering at his commander-in-chief's animation. There seemed to be an almost visible current of excitement electrifying his every movement.

Something was afoot . . . Ah, well, André would most likely have the news when he finally turned up. In the meantime, he felt a greater interest in his own instructions to MacDowell to stop by the Theatre Royal or Amalie's lodgings at least once a day so he would have the earliest news of her arrival. Her landlady had received word to ready her apartment, but no specific date for her coming had been given.

That news, as it happened, came from the lady herself in a brief typical note delivered to him at headquarters. It consisted of a single line, a single question, "Will you dine with me at City Tavern at half after six before the evening cotillion?"

He was there at a quarter past the hour, and his insides all but turned over when he saw her enter the vestibule ten minutes later, his glowing pocket Venus in a gown of pink velveteen, lovelier than all his fondest memories.

Tears sprang into her eyes at the sight of him. Her lips trembled and her voice was tremulous when she uttered his name in a voice of unmistakable love that he had never heard from her before. "Alexander. Oh, Alexander, I did miss you."

He walked towards her, the question of whether he loved or hated more already answered. Her arms were waiting. He felt that he must die if he did not kiss her and that the kiss might be worth the dying; but first there was something that had to be said.

"I love you, Amalie. Will you marry me?"

The early diners at the City Tavern considered they had gotten more than their money's worth that night—a sizzling love scene played out for them while they drank their chowder and ate their mutton or lobster, performed, those not-in-the-know were informed, by one of Sir Henry Clinton's aides, who was a younger son of the Earl of Beaumont, and the famed New York Royal Theater actress, Madame Nostrand.

Amalie neither accepted nor refused him; he was to remember that later. For the moment she was in his arms and he in hers; there seemed to be such communion between them he doubted they could have been closer if he had taken her there on the tavern floor.

He assumed her acquiescence, not in his old arrogant way but because refusal seemed impossible. As he loved her, so she loved him, and whatever differences had separated them in the past had ceased to exist. Or, so he thought.

Chapter Fourteen

New York, October 1780

"The Events of coming within an Enemys posts and of Changing my dress which led me to my present Situation were contrary to my own Intentions as they were to your Orders . . ."

—*From last letter of Major John André to Sir Henry Clinton, dated Sept. 29, 1780 at Tapaan*

THE DRAGOONS' HORSES WERE SO LATHERED, their breathing so labored, that De Lacey held back a reprimand with difficulty. To see good horseflesh so abused . . . but no doubt the private communiqué to Sir Henry Clinton was of great import. He saw to the delivery himself.

Several minutes later a strange guttural cry brought him through the door of the commander-in-chief's office without the ceremony of a knock.

Sir Henry Clinton sat at his desk, grim and white-faced, his eyes puffier than ever in his plump, irritable face. But there was no sign of irritation now, only of a pain almost too great to be borne.

Instinctively Alex sprang to his side.

"Sir Henry?"

"André is taken, De Lacey," said the commander-in-chief on a groan.

"Taken?" Alex repeated dumbly.

"Arrested by the enemy. Oh, my God, he is done for!"

"I don't understand."

"They caught him behind enemy lines out of uniform. Good Christ!" He pounded the desk with his fist in a fury of rage and grief. "I gave him strict orders under no circumstance to leave off the uniform. Now, that hell's fiend Washington has the excuse he needs to destroy him."

That André was head of intelligence-gathering for Clinton, De Lacey had long suspected; that his friend played the spy himself, he had never dreamed.

It was all over headquarters in a matter of minutes, the chief morsel of gossip in every New York tavern and household by the next day.

For over a year André had been dealing with

the American general, Benedict Arnold, on a plan to defect to the British. Their transactions had been conducted through third parties at first, with Arnold not revealing himself until the preliminaries seemed firm. The main business of their negotiations had been the price of treason, which jumped much higher when Arnold's maneuvers gave him the command of West Point, and thus the means to deliver this strategic plum into the hands of the British.

Candles burned all through the night in headquarters at Number One, Broad Way. The shutters were drawn tightly on secret conferences during which frenzied plans were proposed—jettisoned—accepted—and frantic paper work was done as the command of the British war machine concentrated its mighty efforts on the endeavor to save one man's life.

De Lacey contrived a hasty note to Amalie the next day to explain his absence, though he knew the Theatre Royal must be buzzing with the rumors of the fate of its favorite military performer.

Reports came into headquarters almost every hour on the hour.

Arnold, learning of André's capture in the so-called neutral ground, had escaped to the British ship, *Vulture*.

André's place of imprisonment was a close-kept secret.

The arrested officer had been examined,

and at his trial on Friday, the twenty-ninth of September, had made a full and free confession of his activities.

Major John André, having been adjudged guilty of spying, was sentenced to execution by hanging.

An anonymous source believed by some to have been Alexander Hamilton suggested to General Clinton that André might be handed over in exchange for the traitor Arnold. There were men on his staff more than willing; perhaps it was even his own secret inclination, but Sir Henry's honor and conscience could not allow him to countenance such a proposal.

In the face of the British commander's impassioned threats and pleas to Washington of the blood bath that would ensue if André died, the execution was set for the first of October at five P.M.

A half day's delay was granted so that further evidence sent by Sir Henry could be perused. Major-General James Robertson and two other prominent Britishers brought this information from New York, but it proved of no aid to the convicted man.

Major John André—soldier, actor, poet— lamented by friend and foe alike, died on the gallows at high noon on Monday, the second of October. Exercising to the end his courtesy, charm and outward aplomb, he adjusted his own blindfold and the rope about his neck and addressed himself to General Green.

"You will bear me witness that I die like a brave man."

The British army plunged into profound grief and mourning, Sir Henry Clinton's greater than any other. He had lost his chief military aide and head of intelligence, but even more, the young man who had become as dear as a son to him. Remorse and grief mingled with guilt and a savage thirst for vengeance. Let Washington's spies beware now!

The third evening after his friend's hanging, Alex had his first few hours of leisure. The theater was closed, but he took a hackney to Amalie's lodgings, fairly confident that he would find her home. She must know he would come to her as soon as his duty to Sir Henry permitted. André had been her friend, too, he reminded himself, taking the stairs to her apartment two at a time. In mutual expressions of their sorrow, they might both find a little heart's ease.

The landlady had said she was at home, but there was no answer to his first soft knock or his second much louder one. After a moment's wait, he tried the knob, discovered the door open, and without hesitation entered.

He found himself in what seemed to be a small reception parlor, with only one candle standing in its holder on a small table in the corner.

"Amalie," he called out, fearing to frighten her by a sudden appearance.

When there was no answer, he walked into the next room.

There were no candles lit, only the glow of a puny fire to show him the figure huddled at the far end of the room. She sat on a low hassock in front of the fire, back and shoulders humped over, arms embracing her knees and her head bent into the cradle formed by both. She was rocking back and forth, back and forth, in the slow silent eloquence of grief.

"Amalie." He knelt to her, his hand on one of the hunched shoulders. "Amalie, darling."

Her body straightened, she lifted her face to him, and he felt a moment's shock. This was an Amalie he had never seen before, with her face ghostly white in the dim glow of the fire and her eyes puffily red and swollen from long weeping. This was not his strong, sure, lovely, laughing Amalie but a stranger in a torn nightdress and a stained dressing gown with her powdered hair in wild disarray. For the first time he recognized a kinship in her to her sisters . . . there was in her both the sad bitterness of Julianne and the soft melancholy vulnerability of Melrosa.

She had never, since they first met, looked less beautiful, and he had never before loved her so greatly.

He smoothed strands of hair back from her damp face, pressed a kiss on each of the swollen eyelids.

"Beloved," he whispered over and over.

She launched herself at him with such passionate force, he was all but knocked over. Still on his knees, braced to bear the assault of her heaving, twisting body, he tried to comfort her storm of weeping and make sense of the disjointed words she was uttering between deep sobs as she clung to him with both hands digging into the back of his neck like claws.

At last as she quieted a little, he rose to his feet, bringing her with him, willing to endure her stranglehold and the scratches on his neck or anything else that brought her ease.

When the violence of her weeping subsided, he finally made sense of the words she kept repeating over and over, "I am so frightened. Oh, God, oh, Alexander, I am so frightened."

Presently her fingers ceased clawing at his neck and clenched in fists against her breast. She half lay against him, breathing in ragged gasps but making no other sound except an occasional whimper.

After another long while she sighed and lifted her head and said, "I'm sorry, Alex. Forgive me . . . as though you don't have troubles of your own."

"Don't be a fool!" he told her with rough tenderness. "*Your* troubles are mine. Is it André, Amalie?"

Her tears began to fall again, splashing down her cheeks like rain, choking up her voice. "I think of him . . . day and night . . . night and day . . . I s-see him . . . I am afraid

147

to go to sleep . . . he f-fills my dreams . . . he is there, always . . . dangling at the end of a rope." Her hands moved up to her own throat, gripping it convulsively. "A rope, st-strangling the life out of him!"

"Amalie, stop it, stop it!" He shook her till the glazed fanatical light went out of her eyes and the sudden alarming rigor of her body melted into fluid human flesh again.

His arms wrapped her, his hands moved over her in love and comfort. "We are all in pain over André, but you cannot make yourself ill like this. Every soldier knows the risks he takes; John must have been more aware than most of the consequences of acting the—the—"

She lifted her face to him. "The spy?" she whispered.

"Yes, the spy. He said as much in his last letter to Sir Henry. He knew he was to die, and at such a time he tried to ease Clinton's mind of any blame and guilt." With his handkerchief he wiped the last tear stains from her face and stroked the hair back from her forehead. "I have heard the evidence of witnesses to the execution," he told her with kind firmness. "They are all agreed that he died gallantly and quickly. Far more quickly than most soldiers die in battle."

Her only answer was an attack of shivering. He took hold of her chilled hands, then knelt again, rubbing her icy feet. "My God, you are so cold! Let me build up the fire. Or better still, I have a few hours before I must report back to headquarters. Why don't you dress and I will take you out for a light supper. Where is your maid?"

"In Hoboken," said Amalie, sounding more like herself. "She married a farmer's son. And I have not eaten in two days. Only tea." Her hands went to her throat again. "Even the thought of food chokes me. I cannot eat or sleep or—"

He heard hysteria threatening in her voice again and broke in sternly, "Hush! Wait here for me."

He was gone from the room for a few minutes, and when he returned, she was back on her hassock but sitting upright now. She watched him add two heavy logs to the fire; they blazed up suddenly, and she gave a little sigh of pleasure as the heat spread out to her.

"Your landlady is bringing some tea and toast and beef and broth for both of us. Why don't you freshen up a bit," he suggested persuasively, "and we will have a cozy little meal here by the fire."

She nodded apathetically and disappeared into her bedroom. When she returned fifteen minutes later, in a fresh dressing gown, her hair tied loosely back, a small gateleg table had been converted to a dining table and a chair set on either side of it directly in front of the fire. The landlady had already come with her tray and gone.

149

He partook of their meal heartily but did not press her when she could not, content that she swallowed half her bowl of broth and drank two cups of tea. They ate for the most part in silence, but he sensed the language of appeal in the way her left hand lay, palm up, on the table. Again and again he reached over to grip it whole in his or press the fingers painfully. Even as she winced, the gesture seemed to restore her.

After the dishes were removed, he took her into his arms again.

"Can you sleep now, love?" he asked her tenderly.

"Not alone."

He had put the question with no thought of lust or passion. The overwhelming desire he always felt for her was quiescent, subdued from the moment he had entered her rooms by the more overwhelming wish to cherish her, care for her, comfort her.

Not alone. At the implication in those two simple words, scarcely able to believe his ears, he put her a little away from him so he could look down into her face.

"Amalie." With the sudden new rush of desire, his breathing became ragged as hers had been. "Amalie?" he said again . . . hopeful . . . doubtful . . . still disbelieving.

"Don't leave me," she whispered. "I don't want you to leave me."

He swung her up into his arms, holding her tightly against his chest. Her head lay against his shoulder with the long trailing ends of her hair wrapped around his neck.

With a supreme effort of will he gave her one last chance to change her mind. "Do you want me to take you into your bedchamber?"

With one finger she outlined his mouth, his chin, and the gold braid on his jacket. Then she nodded solemnly. Yes.

He felt torn apart, not wanting to take advantage of her yet just plain wanting her! Determined to have no misunderstanding, he questioned her hoarsely. "And do you want me to stay with you?"

"Yes, please."

She sounded like a child accepting a treat, but it was all the invitation he needed.

He walked with her into the bedroom and laid her on the bed. Though he had no doubt that he could keep her warm, he built up the bedroom fire, too, before starting to undress.

Amalie lay quietly beneath a featherbed until he joined her. She seemed eager to burrow back into his arms again and curl up against his naked body, but to his disappointment, she had not taken off her robe and nightdress.

He slipped the robe down from her shoulders and began to kiss bare flesh wherever he could find it.

"You know," he told her between kisses, "we would both be much more comfortable if you would dispose of these garments. They tend to get in the way."

"All right," she agreed in the same child's voice.

"May I help you?"

"Yes, please."

When she was bare, too, she scrambled back into his arms, seemingly so intent, in her panicked need for comfort, on getting inside him that he wondered—grinning in the darkness of the bed curtains even as he fought for control—if she had forgotten that it was supposed to be the other way around.

"Oh, you feel so good, so good. I do love you, Alexander," she sighed, her slender arms around his neck and her bare breasts flattened against his chest.

The total realization came to him that no matter how much she loved him, this was not his passionate Amalie he was holding to him but a frightened little animal scurrying for cover.

Marvelously and miraculously, it did not matter. He loved her enough to give her whatever it was she wanted of him and to accept joyfully whatever little she had to give.

Presently, as he lay over but not quite on her, her knees raised and separated in the most natural way. She welcomed him into her as she had welcomed the touch of his hand. His movements were quiet and controlled; he stroked her shoulders and whispered words of love he had never used before—not to any of the many women—because the words and the women had never before had meaning.

When he had used his body to comfort her and to relieve himself and they lay together, quietly entwined, she said again, "Oh, you feel so good, Alexander."

He kissed her hands and her lips and her breasts. "So do you," he said. "Now sleep, my love, sleep."

In the firelight, with the bedcurtains pulled aside, he saw her smile, a smile that was the Mona Lisa and the Madonna and his Amalie all rolled into one. Then, like the docile child she had become this evening, she closed her eyes.

Alex dozed a little himself, and on waking, saw that she was fast asleep with the lingering trace of that same smile upon her face. He did not think there would be any more nightmares tonight. His heart swelled with a curiously humble pride that this should be so.

Tomorrow, he thought, easing himself out of the bed ever so gently so as not to disturb her, tomorrow she would mourn in a more natural way. But tonight—he pulled on his breeches, his heart, in spite of poor André, singing—tonight his love would sleep.

Chapter Fifteen

Turtle Bay, October 1780

". . . I have every reason to believe the Step which I have taken will in its Consequences have the most happy effect; and will tend to promote His Majestys Service more effectually than an expenditure of a like sum could possably have done in any other way . . . you will not think my Claim unreasonable, when you Consider the Sacrafises I have made, and that the sum is a trifling object to the Public and of Consequence to me . . ."

—Letter from Benedict Arnold
to Sir Henry Clinton
October 18, 1780

THE SIGHT OF GENERAL BENEDICT ARNOLD walking in and out of headquarters as easily as though it were his own command was so sickening to Major Alexander De Lacey that he kept as far away from the man as he could.

Sir Henry might issue orders on the dignity to be accorded him and remind his men that the general had returned from a state of rebellion to his proper loyalty; but Alex and others saw in the American a venal traitor who, to ensure his own greater safety, had imposed on André to remove his uniform.

He missed Amalie achingly, the one night's gentle possession having awakened rather than assuaged his raging desire. But Amalie, at his suggestion, had gone to Turtle Bay, and for her sake, he must be glad.

He had written her every day, twice a day, after their brief bittersweet evening together:

Your sisters are still in Trenton, and Cousin Frederick must be lonely. Your visit would be such a joyous surprise to him, and I would feel so much happier, knowing you were in his care.

I thought I might finally get to see you, my love, but Sir Henry has us on duty day and night and warns that we may expect it to be so for some time. Do go to Turtle Bay, dear heart.

Arnold has arrived, and we are expected to receive him with honor and courtesy. I cannot stomach the man and would face the guns of battle more gladly. We are now to go spy-catching ourselves. Sir Henry is determined to route the enemy's agents from New

155

York and hopes Arnold may be able to help us. I am so happy that you have written to your uncle. I know how gladly he will welcome you.

I am saddened and happy by your news, sad that you will be that many more miles from me, but happy, much happier that you will be at Turtle Bay. With the theater closed and our opportunities to be together reduced to nothing, I would rather, far rather, have you comfortably at Lacey Manor with Cousin Frederick than lonely and sad in your lodgings.

Beloved, I meant to stop by this morning to bid you farewell, but I must go to Staten Island instead. As soon as possible, I will come to Turtle Bay. MacDowell has all my messages for you except the most important one. I love you, Amalie.

Alex hurried through his meetings and arranged his trip back from Staten Island six hours earlier than he was expected. He had high hopes that Sir Henry would give him those six hours off, with the evening thrown in, in which case he would be able to ride out to Lacey Manor to see Amalie.

Even if he could not stay the night, even if they were unable to be private together, still he would see her. For the present—so far had the mighty fallen—just the sight of her would answer his every notion of happiness.

Outside Sir Henry's office he heard the commander-in-chief's voice, loud and bitter, "An Irish tailor and two women; not much of a game bag to exchange for André."

"They may lead us to others, sir." That sounded like Robertson.

He was about to knock briskly when a third voice froze him in his tracks.

"Is it really possible De Lacey has no idea at all about the woman's involvement?"

"Of course he doesn't." To the shameless eavesdropper in the corridor, pretending—in case anyone came by—to have dropped his snuff box, Sir Henry's voice sounded testy now. "He would have come to me."

"He is infatuated with her."

"He is an honorable British officer," Sir Henry snapped, "and a Beaumont."

Robertson's voice asked placatingly, "Is Arnold sure of its being Madame Nostrand?"

"Do you know of another woman who fits the description of a beautiful young actress at the Theatre Royal who is the widow of a rebel officer, a connection—though he doesn't receive her—of Frederick De Lacey's, and a close friend of John André's?"

Major Alex De Lacey, André's other close friend, rose, replaced the snuff box in his pocket, dusted off his breeches, and walked away to his own office.

He sat at his desk for a long time, with his head in his hands.

I am so frightened. Oh God, Alexander, I am so frightened.

He fills my dreams . . . he is there, always . . . dangling at the end of a rope.

Small wonder she had been frightened. With good cause. She had every reason to fear the same fate she may perhaps have had a hand in meting out to André.

She had played them all for fools. All the British officers who languished after her and must have been easy sources of information. Even André. And himself.

Himself, most of all, he decided dispassionately, even as his legs trembled under him and his heart turned to dead-weight within him, and his mind told him that from *this* grief, *this* sorrow there would be no recovery; this burden he would carry all his life long.

An orderly came along, exclaiming in surprise, "Major De Lacey, I didn't know you were back, sir."

He looked up, forced himself to say casually, "I arrived just three minutes ago."

"I believe General Clinton wished to be informed of your return, sir."

"I will go to him at once."

He moved noisily along the corridor so they would surely hear him and rapped loudly at Sir Henry's door.

Sir Henry and the three others in the room all looked at him in what he fancied was guilty surprise. "You are back early, my boy," the commander-in-chief told him.

"Everything went quite smoothly, sir. Here are the dispatches." He handed them over.

Sir Henry broke the seal and gave the papers a cursory look even as he told De Lacey, "I have a small troop assembling under the Colonel here for an important mission—the arrest of the man Arnold believes to be one of Washington's chief spies here in New York— Hercules Mulligan."

"Mulligan? You mean the clothier on Queen Street?"

"You know him?" Sir Henry and the Colonel both spoke together.

"He made up two new uniforms for me before Charleston." He brushed the sleeve of his jacket carelessly. "I believe this is one of them."

"Well, he seems to concoct treason as well as uniforms. I would like you to go along with the Colonel."

"It would be my pleasure, sir. Immediately?"

"We assemble out back in twenty minutes."

De Lacey saluted briskly and walked out with the jaunty step of a soldier relishing an assignment. Once outside, he deliberately twisted a button off the jacket that had been carefully sewn by the man about to be arrested. He then sought out the orderly who had given him instructions to see Clinton, casually showing him the loose threads.

"You know my batman MacDowell? Good. Well, hustle over to my lodgings and tell him to get here on the double with another jacket."

While he waited, pacing around his office, he removed his jacket and placed it on the desk.

Let him be there, he prayed. *Let him get here in time.* There was no doubt in his mind another troop was assembling to pick up Madame Nostrand.

Even as he prayed, he cursed aloud. "Damn you, Amalie! Damn you to hell!"

Fifteen minutes later, just as the Major was giving up hope, the batman came stomping in, a jacket over his arm.

De Lacey closed the door firmly and allowed himself to be helped into the jacket. He had only three minutes left. Mindful of how he himself had eavesdropped outside Sir Henry's office, he pitched his voice low.

"MacDowell, I cannot give you orders about an errand I want you to undertake for me. It is not in the army's interest as well as being potentially dangerous."

"Is it in your interest, sir?"

The Major looked across at his batman.

"Aye," he said in simple, unconscious mimicry.

"I'm your man, sir," said MacDowell.

"Take Jupiter then . . . he's my best horse after Highland. Here—you may need money. Get to Turtle Bay—to Lacey Manor as fast as you can. Keep yourself inconspicuous; see

Madame Nostrand *privately* and warn her that Arnold has exposed her to Sir Henry. She is in danger of arrest and must get away at once."

The batman's face remained impassive. "I will remember it all, sir, never fear."

"If she should be away from the house, then say what I have told you to Mr. De Lacey. He may be shocked, but he will help her."

"Not a doubt of it, sir."

"Get back to my lodgings as fast as you can afterward. I don't want any longer absence than possible noticed, in case there should be questions asked later."

"I'm on my way, sir."

"Godspeed, and thank you, MacDowell."

He waited one minute while the batman slipped away, then went outside to join the Colonel and his little troop.

Mulligan's arrest went off without a hitch. The cheerful Irishman appeared to regard the whole episode as an hilarious joke.

"You British are always arresting me," he complained good-humoredly. "I wish you would stop wasting your time and mine and let me get on with me business"—he paused a fraction of a moment and his eyes twinkled challengingly at the Colonel—"of making clothes."

He then looked appraisingly at Alex De Lacey. "The uniform suits you well, Major. A fine job I did, and it's pleased I am that it wasn't ruined by bullet holes."

"I'm even more pleased about that, Mr. Mulligan," Alex answered pleasantly.

In the seconds that their eyes met and held, Alex became certain that Arnold was right about *this* man. But later, when Mulligan was under lock and key, it appeared there was no hard evidence against him—only Arnold's suspicions.

"We'll question him round the clock if we must," growled Smith of Intelligence, "but the fellow's a wily serpent, not a man of honor like André. He's slipped through our hands before."

De Lacey bit back the retort that it might have been better if André had been less flamboyantly honorable and more serpentlike himself. He might then have been a live soldier rather than a mourned martyr.

Following the arrest there was another staff conference from which he was excused so that he could attend to a large pile of Sir Henry's correspondence. Glancing at the file, he saw that it was heavy enough to keep him occupied well into the night.

He studied it with assumed interest, asked a few questions, made a few notes, pretending not to understand that he was being kept away from the chief business of headquarters that night—the apprehension and examination of other spies!

His apparent unawareness, he decided grimly, as he walked towards his own office, with the sergeant who would act as his secretary just behind him, matched any acting performance of André's. He might, he thought bitterly, make a good spy himself.

It was a long day and a longer night, but when he finally was able to go back to his rooms, MacDowell was there waiting for him.

He took one look at the Major's haggard face and reached out to touch his shoulder, not as master to man, but as comrade and soldier.

"Never fret, sir; she's safe away."

"You spoke to her?"

"No, only to Mr. De Lacey."

"Even if she got away from Lacey Manor, how can you be sure she is safe? There hasn't been time enough to be sure."

"She never went to Lacey Manor, sir. Mr. De Lacey had never even heard from her that she proposed to visit him. A letter was slipped under the door last night—no one knows how —from some place in the Jerseys—Hybroken, I think . . ."

"Hoboken?"

"Ay, that was the name. It seems she left New York two days ago on a fishing boat." MacDowell hesitated. "She must have had some idea that Headquarters was getting suspicious."

"Headquarters was," the Major told his man grimly, "and *I* supplied her with the idea. It seems everyone was getting suspicious of *her* except her nearest and dearest, including a fool like me."

"That's plain nonsense, sir," said MacDowell with his typical Scots candor. "You may have been fooled, sir, but you were no' a fool," he added with blunt kindness. "There's a vast difference between the two."

Alexander gave a short and bitter laugh. "I'm afraid the rest of the army doesn't agree with you."

"The rest of the army forgets that Major André, as canny a man as there was at Headquarters, was no more suspicious of her than you." His voice softened. "There was a letter for you, sir, enclosed with the one to her uncle. I would have brought it with me, Major, but Mr. De Lacey—he said, no, he would bring it himself or send it on to you later. In case I was stopped, he thought it would put me under suspicion to be carrying letters from her."

The Major nodded agreement. "My cousin acted correctly. You endangered yourself enough for me as it was." It was his turn to put a hand on his batman's shoulder. "Thank you, MacDowell, I shan't forget. Get to bed now. God knows you have had a long hard day."

MacDowell opened the door that led to his own small quarters, hesitated a few seconds, then turned back.

"Major De Lacey, sir?"

"Yes?" Alexander said impatiently.

"Excuse my saying so, sir," the batman told him in anything but the humble tones of someone suing for pardon, "but I think there is something you are overlooking. The lady didn't deceive you for personal gain. She was doing *her* duty as she saw it."

Alex walked over to the single window and stood there for a long time, looking out but not seeing the darkness of the streets or the specks of light on the distant river.

"Thank you, MacDowell," he said presently, and the soldier was relieved to see some of the tension go out of the major's back and shoulders.

Chapter Sixteen

Turtle Bay, October 1780

"I do not think I shall ever wish for a letter again."

—*Catherine Morland*
in *Northanger Abbey*

THE PACKET THAT ARRIVED BY MESSENGER from Lacey Manor contained not just one letter but three. From constant reading, re-reading, interpretation, and attempts to find between the lines meanings that were not written down, Alexander De Lacey was soon in a fair way to knowing all three by heart.

My dear Cousin Alex,

To say that I am sorely troubled would be to Understate the Perturbasion of my Mind. It still Passes my Belief that the daughter of Jacob van Raalte—a man as Stawnchly Loyal to the King as any man in New York colony—could have Played the Part now A-tributed to her. Even when she Wed an American Officer, I made nothing of it, because I considered her Marriage one of Expediencey rather than of Politicks. Amalie allways Avowed that she Despized Politicks.

Despite the Severall Years gone bye that I have not seen her, Amalie has allways held a Place in my Heart, from which even now I cannot Find in me the Strenth to Disslodge Her.

If it is not in your Power to Forgive her, dear Alex, at least I Pray you try to Beleeve, as I am Endevoring to Do, that she acted from the Sinsere Dicktates of her Conshence.

I enclose the Two Letters that turned up on my Door Step, one Addressed to me and one to you. I had Intended to bring them to Manhattan myself, but I am not well and my poor Julianne, who came Home to this Dire News, Is Prostrait. I suspeckt she Suffers Remorse, thinking that if she had been less Flint-Harted t'wards Amalie, her Sister would have Stayed with us and not Gotten Involved in these Sordid Mens Conserns.

I know not. Amalie was Ever a Law Unto Herself.

Come to us when you can, Distrawt tho we

be, knowing Yourself Ever Wellcome at the home of

> *Your devoted cousin,*
> *Frederick De Lacey*

Dear Uncle Frederick,

If the truth has not already been told you, then I must Confess it to you myself, since I reveal nothing that is not now known. My Acting at the Theatre, all my other Activitys have been a cloak for the Nature of my True Work, which has been to gather Intelligence for the American side.

It is because of this, not due to Julianne, that I would not come to Lacey Manor, dear Uncle. I could not live in your home, accepting your Love and Bounty the while I worked against All your most Cherished Beliefs. It is my Deepest Regret, Uncle Frederick, that we are on Opposed Sides of this Struggle, but so it must be. As you followed your Conscience, so must I follow Mine.

I am Forced to flee for my Safety's Sake since the cursed Traitor Arnold is arrived in New York, but when the War is over, how Happily I will come to you, in Victory or in Defeat, if you are still willing to Receive me.

> *Your loving Amalie*

P.S. The Sealed Enclosure is for Major De

Lacey if you will be so Kind as to send it to him in New York.

My Dear Alexander,

What is there left for me to say now that you have been Informed what you must think is the Worst of me? I used you, yes. I Deceived you, true. But I cannot apologize, neither can I ask you to forgive me—though I know with great Sadness that you will Disagree—because, by my own Code of Right and Wrong, my dear, I have nothing to Apologize for, nothing for which I require Forgiveness.

We are both Patriots, Alexander. Sadly, we are Patriotic in differing Causes. You are English, I am American. You wear a Uniform and fight for your Country. I wore an Actor's Mask and fought for Mine.

Now I must Flee so that I will be Safe to fight another Way, another Day.

I ask you to Believe two things. The first, that I had not any part in sending André to his death. Long before I met you, he was my Dear and well-loved Friend. If I had had to make the Decision to Deliver him up—ah well, I thank the Good Lord I was never put to that Awful Test.

What I ask, secondly, may Tax your Credulity even more, but it is the simple Truth. I am not so good an Actress as to have Simu-

*lated my Feelings for you. I did love you
Truly, Alexander. I still do. God help me, I am
afraid I always Shall.*

                                    Amalie

After long thought, Alex took the three letters to Sir Henry's office and placed them
before the commander-in-chief. He thought
that he owed it to Amalie, to Frederick, to
André, and even to himself.

Clinton read the letters through with fur-
rowed brow.

"You have my sympathy, Alexander," he
made unexpected response. "I have never
doubted your loyalty, your integrity, or your
intelligence." He smiled wryly. "If I did, I
would have to doubt my own. The lady misled
me too. Tell me, Alexander"—he scratched
his chin—"Your situation right now—I know
—is quite difficult. Would you like me to write
to Cornwallis and try to effect a transfer for
you to his staff?"

De Lacey's face brightened. "I would be
most grateful, sir. You are right . . . to leave
New York—just now—would be an object
with me."

He refrained from mentioning that he was
fully aware that a British staff officer known
to have fallen in love with an American spy
must be an embarrassment to his commander-in-chief. A transfer to Cornwallis
in the South would gratify everyone. Except,

perhaps, Lord Cornwallis. Let the fiction be preserved, however, that the change would be made solely for his own benefit.

Sir Henry handed back his aide's letters and tapped some pages lying on his desk. "I have had a letter of my own this day," he said, smiling bleakly. "From Arnold here in New York, dated on the eighteenth of the month, which is to say, two weeks after I was informed of the—the execution of André. He wastes no time in regrets but gets straight to the heart of the matter. Pray God he may be equally as direct in battle."

Sir Henry then read aloud in a voice seemingly devoid of feeling:

"In the Conference which I had with Major André, He was so fully Convinced of the reasonableness of my proposal of being allowed Ten thousand pounds Sterling for my Services, Risque, and the loss which I should Sustain in Case a discovery of my Plan should oblige me to take Refuge in New York before it could be fully carried into Execution, that he assured me, tho he was Commissioned to promise me Only six thousand pounds Sterling, He would use his influence and recommend it to your Excellency to allow the sum I proposed, and from his State of the matter He informed me He had no doubt Your Excellency would accede to the proposal . . ."

171

"Faugh!" He interrupted himself to drop Arnold's letter onto his desk, brushing his fingertips distastefully, as though they had been contaminated by the brief touch of the paper. De Lacey had been cursing low and fluently through most of the reading.

"What will you do, sir?"

"Do?" Sir Henry straightened in his chair. "I shall do my utmost for him," he said curtly, "then use the man as best I can, since we have already paid a heavy price to secure his services for the Crown. We are none of us individuals in this struggle, Alexander," he reminded his aide. "If we were, I should be home in England, and you—might you not be in the arms of your actress and the hell with political differences?"

"Perhaps," said Alexander, his smile as desolate as his commander's. "But you are right, sir. We are neither of us free to choose."

"I will write to Cornwallis by the first dispatches that go out," Sir Henry said in kind reaffirmation and dismissal.

Major De Lacey bowed, saluted, and withdrew to inform MacDowell that they might soon be leaving for the South.

The preparations that both began to make, however, were destined to be wasted. Long before an answer arrived from Lord Cornwallis, a transport ship from Plymouth, with some of Sir Henry's long-awaited reinforcements, docked in New York. The sealed government pouch delivered to General Clinton contained instructions from the highest level of government for the commander to facilitate and speed the return to England of Major Alexander De Lacey. The same order was given under the royal seal.

There was also a letter to De Lacey, written from Beaumont by Lord Donald Graham-Worth, his pompous, kindly brother-in-law.

My dear Alexander,

It is my painful duty to send you news of a most distressing and alarming nature. Would that anyone else could do it, but alas, there is no one, only your dear mother, and she, poor lady, is in no fit case to make the effort.

Your brother Edward lately purchased a new horse, a wild chestnut with so many nasty tricks even your father advised against it. Edward, as you know, has always been the most amiable young man on any subject except his horses. He was determined to master the chestnut, quite correctly named Satan.

Last week, when he thought he had succeeded, the animal returned to the stable with his saddle empty.

Some farmers brought Edward home on a hurdle. He has remained Unconscious ever since. The Injuries to his head and to his back are so severe as to leave no hope of his

recovery. The local doctors and two special-
ists brought from London all Concur in this
opinion.

Dorothea and I were spending the winter
at Beaumont. Your sister, as you know, was
eight months gone with child and had taken
it into her head that if she had her lying-in at
Beaumont we would have the girl she desired
so greatly after our two fine boys.

When Edward was carried in, there was
much weeping and wailing among the ser-
vants, and several cried out, "He is dead! He
is dead!" Sinking under this conviction,
Dorothea fell to the ground in a swoon, so
that your mother knew not which of her
children to attend to first and was well nigh
distracted.

Dorothea went into premature labor, and I
regret to inform you that the child born to us
that night, who was indeed a girl, lived not
above six hours. Your sister is much affected,
as are we all, by this added grief.

Your father and I, at the time of Edward's
accident, were riding the estate together
and paying some tenants visits. We were
summoned home to the scene of confusion
and tragedy I have described to you.

My dear Alexander, how I wish I could
spare you, but there is yet worse to be told.

All that night your father went back and
forth from the invalid bed of one child to that
of the other, but when the physicians from
London told him that there was no hope at all

for Edward, he was completely overcome, having never until then lost hope of a miracle.

During the night he suffered a paralytic seizure on his left side, which has left him severely incapacitated. He can hardly walk, his speech is sadly garbled, and he is mostly confined to bed.

My dear Alexander, it is with great sorrow that I must tell you that the doctors consider him as near to death as your beloved brother. Indeed, we all feel that it is only the hope of your return that now keeps him alive.

I do not know whether you were as yet informed, but settlements were being prepared and your brother's formal betrothal to the Lady Rona, youngest daughter of the Duke of Falsorth, was to have been announced at Christmas.

With Edward's and his own death so imminent, and you thousands of miles away, your life at risk in the American rebellion, your father is in a state of painful anxiety about the succession.

To put it plainly, Alexander, he wants you home at once. Your cousin Henry has already enlisted the aid of the King in effecting your immediate release from the Army.

Even more, your father wants you wed, with the prospect of an heir. To be blunt, Falsorth and Lady Rona are prepared in this situation to change the settlement agreements so that you take the place of Edward. I *can assure you, having seen her on numerous occasions, that Falsorth's daughter is a lady of great beauty and refinement. Her breeding, of course, is impeccable.*

You will soon be Earl of Beaumont, Alex. For all we both know, you may even unhappily be so as you read these words. I know I need not remind you of your duty to your name and family, but I implore you—and this is your mother's most ardent request— to come home and take up your duties or, if he still be alive, to comfort your father's last days.

> *Your devoted friend and brother,*
> *Donald Graham-Worth*

Chapter Seventeen

Turtle Bay, November, 1780

"C. J. is again in New York, and entering into business as heretofore, and you may soon I hope receive his dispatches."

—From a New York spy in March 1781
to Benjamin Tallmadge of the American
Secret Service

JULIANNE VAN RAALTE IN HER NEAT QUAKER-gray gown, with a fresh white cotton apron and a snowy linen cap, was bustling about the large comfortable·room next to the kitchen, which Frederick had converted from a parlor to an estate office. There was a convenient and necessary side door leading directly from the office to a bricked long walk between the main house and the farm buildings.

Frederick came down the rear stairway and appeared in the doorway just as Julianne set a tray of mugs on the big Dutch sideboard alongside a pile of pewter plates.

"Everything is ready in the kitchen, Uncle," she told him cheerfully. "I have two platters of cold meats." She began to count on her fingers. "One each of cheeses, bread, and biscuits. Plenty of cold beer." She shivered slightly. "The wine is chilled, too, though on a night like this, I should think my hot mulled cider would be in greater demand. Does it still rain?"

"In torrents, and the wind is high. A hard night for travel, though on the other hand, there will be fewer people abroad to be curious." He walked over to the fireplace and warmed first his hands and then, flipping up his jacket, his nether side. "I am glad this is the last time for a long time," he told her cheerfully, puffing at his inevitable clay pipe.

"I, too." She clasped her hands nervously beneath her chin. "Sometimes I feel the veriest coward, Uncle," she confessed to him.

He crossed quickly from his comfortable spot near the fire over to the sideboard. His hands pushed hers away, lifting up her chin. "Coward, indeed!" he scoffed, then added softly, "Oh, thou of stout heart. Would we had a dozen more like you."

He kissed both sallow cheeks, which warmed to the admiration in his voice, just as a loud commotion sounded in the hallway above them.

Julianne said apprehensively, "It is too early."

"I know." He frowned, laying his pipe on the mantel. "And they know better than to use the front entrance. I had best go up. You wait here just in the event . . ." A nod of his head indicated the side door.

Julianne waited, fretting herself into a fever. The seven or eight minutes until Federick's return seemed to stretch out to a good half hour.

At the sight of his troubled face, her heart gave a leap of fright. "What is it?"

"Alexander De Lacey is here."

"Alexander," breathed Julianne, every vestige of color leaving her face. "What would bring him from New York this time of night and in such weather?"

"There was no time to inquire. He came on horseback and was soaked to the skin. I sent him to undress in the chamber he always uses and promised to send up a hot bath. But how—with the house servants all out?"

"Old Abel and Sarey can help me fill the tub and carry it up," she planned swiftly. "We would never have to worry about them."

Frederick nodded. Old Abel and Sarey had been his father's slaves, given freedom by his father's will. They were as much members of the family as any De Lacey.

Still, the lack of servants was only one problem.

"Our men will be here by the time Alexander's bath is over," he reminded her worriedly, "and when he comes down from the bedchamber, even if I stay in the library with him rather than here, he may get wind of and wonder at so many comings and goings."

"Then what we must devise," Julianne told him promptly, "is a way to ensure that Alexander stays in his bedchamber after he bathes. It should not be too difficult to persuade him that he is hungry and weary," she mused. "A tray could be brought up to him there."

"He may feel he should sit downstairs with *me*."

"*You* have not been well, Uncle, remember? The news about my sister Amalie was such a blow as you have not yet recovered from. The physician wants you early in your bed each night, not arguing politics or playing chess."

Frederick's brow cleared. "It might serve. Do you think you can convince him?"

"Needs must when the devil drives," she said airily, then stood on her toes to kiss his cheek. "Don't worry so, Uncle. I promise you, I shall contrive. Let me first discover, if I can, why he is here so unexpectedly and then see to the tub. Do you stay down here and never fret if I am a long time returning. The cider is simmering over the hearth, and the platters are laid out in the storeroom."

A few minutes later, standing outside the chamber always given to Alexander, her heart was knocking so fiercely against her ribs she marveled that he could not hear it as easily as he did her soft tap upon the door.

"Come in."

She walked in and found Major Alexander De Lacey sitting in the four-poster with the coverlet drawn up to his waist, obviously as naked below as he was above.

"Good heavens!" She glanced without particular modesty at the bare chest and shoulders. "You will catch your death of cold. Get beneath the blankets at once. I will have a tub of hot water prepared immediately."

"I don't need one. I toweled myself vigorously, and I am quite warm. And good evening to you, too, Cousin Julianne. I see that you have not changed in the least."

"Indeed?"

"We have not met for quite some time, and how typical of you promptly to start bawling arbitrary directions for my health and welfare, unlike the usual useless, well-brought-up young lady, who instead makes polite and meaningless inquiries about both."

She ignored the slightly satiric compliment and continued to probe. "Are you hungry, Major?"

"Ravenous!"

"I shall prepare a tray immediately. Would you mind very much, Cousin Alex, eating your meal up here?"

"If you would lend me some clothes of Cousin Frederick's, so that I can descend respectably clad, I need not put you to so much trouble."

"You would rather be doing me a service, Cousin Alexander," she told him coaxingly. "The truth of the matter is that Uncle has not been at all well. He is a little troubled with heart pains, you know—"

"No, I did not know."

"And the shock of Amalie—" She saw the bare torso stiffen and allowed her voice to trail off artistically.

"He is under doctor's orders to retire quite early at night, but if you come down," she explained apologetically, "there would be no getting him to his bed early. You know he is as stubborn as a Dutchman. There would be talk of politics and—and other unsettling things, perhaps a game of chess, some wine, which he is strictly forbidden . . . but if I could tell him that *you* are too weary to leave your room tonight . . ."

"You may tell him exactly what will aid your purpose, Cousin Julianne, though I find it hard to believe you need such subterfuge. You are a fairly stubborn Dutchwoman yourself."

She came over and patted one bare broad shoulder as sexlessly as though he were eight instead of eight and twenty. "Do rest now," she urged, raising his hackles as she had consistently managed to do at their every meeting over the years. "Get under the blankets and keep warm until I return."

In the open doorway, with her hand still on the knob, she turned back to him. "Is there any reason you are here so unexpectedly on such a stormy night?" she asked. "I think Uncle Frederick was worried that something untoward had happened."

"It was not storming when I left headquarters. I would have hired a carriage if I had anticipated such rain, but I thought to save time on horseback, there was so little left in which to make my farewells."

"F-farewells?"

"I am going home."

"Home," she repeated rather stupidly.

"To England. There is a packet departing New York at dawn the day after this next one. I must be on it by tomorrow evening."

"I will tell Uncle Frederick," said Julianne in her usual calm emotionless voice. "He will be so pleased you were able to pay us this last visit."

When she descended the two flights of stairs, there were two men sitting with Frederick, and the room was wreathed with their pipe smoke. The older of the two nodded a curt greeting; the younger seized her by the shoulders and kissed her firmly on the lips.

She smiled faintly and shook her head at him.

"Uncle?"

Frederick moved a little aside with her, and

she quickly sketched in her conversation with his cousin.

"I am going to prepare a tray for both of us and take it up."

"Both of you?"

"I shall eat with him. It will absorb his attention until the others arrive and you get rid of them all. He will expect you to retire early after what I said about your health."

"And you, my dear?" he asked gently.

"I? Oh, I shall smile politely and say goodbye, Uncle. Remember, I am Julianne, I have no feelings. Only Melrosa and Amalie have— have—Speaking of my sisters, have you told them?" She nodded at the men.

"I am waiting until they are all four here; then I will make it quite clear that I will not change my mind. Or permit you to change yours. It is decided. The Triple Ring is dissolved until the threat from Arnold is over. Amalie and Melrosa must stay in Jersey, and *you* will definitely not go to New York. I am unwell, and I need my dear Julianne here at Lacey Manor to take care of me."

Chapter Eighteen

Turtle Bay, November 1780

"There is scarcely a virgin to be found in the part of the country they* have pass'd thro'."

—Thomas Nelson to Thomas Jefferson
January 1777

*the British Army

SOME QUARTER OF AN HOUR LATER THE DOOR OF Alexander's room was flung open. "Here. Put these on," said Julianne's voice, though Julianne herself did not appear. Instead, a gray-clad arm snaked out, tossing what seemed to be a bundle of rags at him. Reaching up, Alexander caught the bundle—a flannel nightshirt and a light wool dressing gown.

A few moments later Julianne staggered in,

her shoulders weighted down by the burden of a huge round silver tray.

Alexander, who had just struggled into the nightshirt and found it much too tight and short, restrained his first impulse to leap up and help her.

"This—this garment is ludicrous. It is straining at the chest and barely reaches my knees."

Julianne eased the tray onto the far side of the bed and wriggled her aching shoulder blades.

"Your knees are hidden under the blankets, Major," she told him tartly, "and so far as I can see"—she came round and bent slightly over him—"your chest is suffering no damage. How strange." She bent lower, and the middle fingers of her right hand moved in widening spirals inside the gaping nightshirt. "Unpowdered, your hair is so straight and dark. I would hardly have expected your chest hair to be such a light brown color or so curly."

With any other woman, he would have considered both words and gesture an invitation, or at the very least, blatant provocation. But Julianne van Raalte was like no other woman, he reminded himself, uncomfortably aware that the light cool touch of her fingers had affected him as though she were a quite ordinary member of her sex.

Julianne, utterly unselfconscious, had moved back to the tray and was spreading a large checked linen square across his lap and another right alongside him.

"Are you going to put on Uncle Frederick's dressing gown?" she asked, plucking it off the bed between them as she sat down.

"Am I eating in or out of bed?"

"In."

"Then I am not."

She balled up the dressing gown, tossed it across to the nearest chair and carefully spread a second cloth over her own skirts. He noticed for the first time that she had discarded both her customary apron and the lace fichu that usually preserved the modesty of her gown. Nor was she wearing her spectacles or perennial spinsterish cap.

Something else was different. He studied her carefully and finally realized what it was. The two mouse-colored braids usually coiled around her head and mostly hidden under the cap were now hanging over her shoulders, much thicker and more lustrous than they had ever seemed and—most surprising—tied frivolously at the ends with silver ribbons.

Julianne plunked a pewter plate on her lap, then selected a slice of beef, and with her fingers, folded it into a crust of bread.

Her teeth crunched down. "You will have to help yourself," she told him with her mouth full. "I'm hungry too."

He imitated her gesture, selecting a larger slice of bread and adding cheese between two layers of beef.

"Mm, this is good."

"Mm, yes."

Having finished and, to his amusement, licked her fingers daintily, like a cat, she spooned some relishes into a cup, which she handed across to him along with a fork. "Here, try the pickled beets and cucumbers. They're delicious. A secret van Raalte recipe. Would you like a cup of tea—China—or some of my hot—?"

"Mulled cider," he finished for her. "D'you know, Cousin Julianne, on my death bed, if I smelled cinnamon and apples, I would be certain I would find you there hovering betwixt heaven and hell, tempting me back to life with hot mulled cider? And did you not tell me I was supposed to serve myself?"

She shrugged. "Old customs die hard. I tell you what"—she placed another slice of bread on her plate—"why don't *you* play gallant and pour the cider for both of us?"

He did so, awkwardly, spilling a little from the pitcher onto the tray and a bit more over her skirt when he tried to slip the handle of the mug off his fingers onto hers.

She gave a shriek and a little leap in the air, and the mug slipped entirely out of his hands.

"Ow!"

"Jesus Christ!"

"Oooh."

"Are you burned, Julianne? Did I hurt you?"

"No, thank God, fortunately it's cooled quite a bit since I brought it up. I'm just so w-wet. It tickles," she lamented, then with superb nonchalance, lifted up the hem of her skirt, gathering plate, mug, and the remains of her soggy bread into a heap, which she stood and emptied into the Delft chamberpot from beneath the bed.

Disregarding the shock in his bulging eyes and open mouth as he watched her, she unbuttoned and stepped out of her gown, brushed off and shook out her lacy petticoats —far prettier than her dress—and calmly plucked her uncle's dressing gown from off the chair and slipped it on.

"I knew this would come in handy," she told Alexander complacently as she tied the sash about her waist, with an extra knot to make sure it held. She pulled the collar decorously around her throat and returned to her spot on the bed, spreading petticoats and the skirt of the dressing gown wide, and curling her legs beneath her in a most unladylike and even more unJuliannelike manner.

"I think I would like more bread and beef," she told him gaily. "Would you, too? But from now on, *I* will do the serving and the pouring."

"In that case, I will have more of everything too." He held out his cup. "You are right. The pickled beets and cucumbers are delicious."

They looked at each other and simultaneously broke out into wild, uncontrollable laughter. The bed rocked with their mirth, and the contents of the tray trembled.

"Stop it! Now stop it!" Julianne said finally, wiping her eyes with a corner of Frederick's dressing gown. "Unless you want to sleep tonight on sheets that are damped with cider."

"God forbid," said Alex piously and promptly went off into another paroxysm.

Julianne, already pouring the cider, tried to steady her shaking hands as she besought him, "D-don't. P-please d-don't, C-c-cousin. N-no m-more."

Alexander reached out to rescue the swaying pitcher, and his sudden movement proved too much for the strained seams of Frederick's nightshirt. With an ominous tearing sound, the sleeves came loose from the shoulders and the sides separated as far as the eye could see.

Julianne, with a high hiccuping giggle, let go of the pitcher, which, fortunately, when it smashed down, landed unbroken on the tray. Less fortunately, half its contents spilled out and sprayed both the bed and the helplessly hysterical duo, who continued to rock back and forth in uncontrollable convulsions of mirth.

"Oh, God! Oh, God!" Julianne held onto her stomach. "I can't bear any more. I didn't know l-laughing could hurt so. Cousin, for the love of Heaven, stop!"

"Anything to oblige a lady."

Before she could even register his sudden change in voice and mood, her shoulders were seized. His lips were on hers, feather-light at

190

first, in a kiss meant to gently persuade her that this was a sweetly-shared cure for their common hysterics.

Somewhere along the way, something changed. His grip on her shoulders kept her immovable; she was pulled across the disordered tray, with the dampness seeping through her petticoats, a piece of cutlery sticking into one hip and a cup handle stabbing against her breast.

His lips were no longer soft or persuasive but fastened powerfully, possessively onto her mouth and, with the same strength but by some unknown agency, her arms seemed somehow to have gotten entangled around his neck. There was a kind of desperate urgency in their embrace; the sweat of passion, the salt of tears, and the sweet stickiness of cider in their kisses.

He broke away first.

"Oh, Christ! Damn, Julianne, I'm sorry."

She gathered up her skirts and dignity in one fell swoop and descended from the bed with all the stateliness of a duchess.

"I should think," she said, "a gentleman of such vast experience as yourself would know that it could only compound the affront to express regret for what we just did. *I* have no intention of apologizing to *you*."

"Of course not. It was my fault," he said, taking all the blame like a gentleman.

"There wasn't any fault involved," Julianne declared loftily. "I regret if the experience fell

191

short of your expectations. For my part, I enjoyed it prodigiously."

The chuckle that started in his throat ended in another prolonged roar of laughter. Julianne stood over him, this time only smiling primly.

"If you aren't the damnedest unexpected girl!" he said finally wiping his eyes. "What the hell do we do about this tray?"

"I shall leave it in on the table in the hallway to be taken care of tomorrow," Julianne decided after a moment's thought. "I can hardly wander through the house looking like this." An airy wave of her hand indicated her wet petticoats and the soaked dressing gown.

"I would carry it for you like a gentleman, but"—he smiled at her engagingly—"I am even less able than you, if the decencies are to be preserved, to dare show myself."

He did, however—keeping a wary eye on the gaping pieces of his garment—manage to heft up the tray into her outstretched hands.

He heard the thump and the clatter as it was deposited on the hall table, then footsteps and the opening and closing of doors. He wondered, with a strange feeling of expectation, if Julianne was planning to return and felt a relief he did not even try to analyze a little later when she came marching back.

The dressing robe was gone, replaced by another of her Quaker-gray gowns, and she was carrying a large pitcher ornamented with red and yellow Dutch tulips.

"I brought you some water for washing from my own room," she said as she walked over to the commode and started filling his wash basin. With her back to him, she said casually as she poured, "Your going home is a great surprise. Uncle Frederick will miss you sorely. It's rather sudden, isn't it? Is Sir Henry leaving, too? Do you go as part of his staff?"

"No, it's personal leave, though I shall sell out now. My father is dying."

She whirled around in dismay.

"And my brother too."

"Oh, my dear—Cousin."

"It seems that, if I am not already Earl of Beaumont, all too soon I shall be."

Seeing the bleak despair in his eyes, she set down her pitcher and instinctively moved near to the bed, yearning to offer the consolation he wanted, though not from *her*.

"I am so sorry, Cousin Alexander," she told him softly. "Perhaps it is not so dire as you fear . . . miracles have happened. . . ."

He was not even listening. "My father is desperate that there be heirs for Beaumont," he was saying, half to himself. "The succession is everything, and the bride is conveniently handy."

"The—bride?"

"Lady Rona Falsworth."

"You will marry her?"

193

"I have little choice."

"Loving my—Amalie, you will marry this—this lady?" she repeated incredulously.

"Loving Amalie! What good have I gotten out of loving Amalie? She is gone, fled to the arms of the American Army. She never intended to have me; I was useful to her."

"Alexander, you fool!"

"Not so much a fool as I was with Amalie," he answered drearily. "The Lady Rona is beautiful, I am told, and respectable and well-bred. *She* would never act on the stage or make a public spectacle of us or involve me in spying against my country."

"Or make you wildly and deliriously happy?"

"The happiness was too brief and the price paid was too high."

"Alexander, you fool!" she said again. And then, "I feel sorry for you," she told him in a low sad voice and quietly left the room.

When the door closed behind her, he ripped off the torn nightshirt and tossed it into a corner. He got up and stalked naked across the room to clean himself at the commode.

As he returned to the bed, he kicked over a footstool and hobbled back to the four-poster, swearing loudly and nursing his toes.

In this undignified posture, half-lying, backside up, one leg extended, Julianne found him when she returned.

"You had better get under the blankets," she said in her ordinary prosaic manner, as though the sight of a naked man, bottom up, was no novel thing.

"Will you stop ordering me around!" he snapped even as he followed her suggestion and slid under, then down on the pillows.

"I was planning to join you there. Would *that* be too arbitrary of me?" she asked him quite meekly.

"Julianne!" He bolted upright in the bed, clutching the coverings to him in the age-old gesture of a virtuous vestal.

She had changed again, out of the Quaker-gray and into a floating, flowered dressing gown, bordered at the hem and wrists and throat with little lace bows. He gulped deep in his throat. A flowing, flowered gown and apparently nothing else.

He wanted her. God, how he wanted her, but she . . .

"Julianne, do you understand what . . . know what you're doing?"

She smiled by way of answer and started untying the multitude of little lace bows. Then she dropped the gown onto the floor and moved just enough for the firelight to reveal her completely.

"God in Heaven!" he said, not profanely, but with reverence.

He had once seen the statue of the Italian Venus, and here she was, a miniature version, in all her lifelike perfection. Who could have believed that all these years *this* had been hidden beneath the Quaker-gray?

He moved over to make room for her as she slipped into the bed beside him.

"Are you a virgin?" he asked abruptly.

He had always believed her to be one, and of the most dedicated and spinsterish variety. Though it hardly seemed possible now, he had to know.

"Does it matter?"

"I don't want to hurt you."

She threw back her head and laughed out loud. "My dear Cousin," she told him mockingly, "I was in Trenton when your gallant army marched through. They left few virgins in their wake." Before he could answer, she reached up and pulled him down to her. "Why don't you stop talking and kiss me again?"

"In a minute. Julianne, you do understand what I just told you. I am going home to marry. I have nothing to offer you but—"

"You can offer me what I want, which is this one night. I have wanted that *and* you— does that surprise you?—since the very first time I set eyes on you."

She laughed softly at the astonishment on his face.

"I have had to be very patient. After all, I was the plain sister, the one that nobody noticed. It was Amalie you fell in love with, naturally. She dazzled you completely; I expected her to. I expected you to be bewitched by her beauty and intrigued by her independence; but in the end she did betray you, just as I knew she would."

Her fingertips spiraled across his chest in the same way they had much earlier. Then she suddenly buried her face in the curly light brown hair of his chest and tugged at it with her teeth. When she lifted her head, she was sweetly smiling again. "I knew Melrosa came next in your affections," she told him caressingly. "How could she not? All that simple loveliness and the lost innocence that caught at everyone's heart—mine, yours, Uncle Frederick's, the servants? And there was I, the dull sister, the quiet sister, the homely one who served all the household. How could you know, any of you, that all the while I was watching and waiting and hugging my wonderful secret to me?"

"What secret?" he asked her hoarsely.

"That I knew you were meant to be here with me like this. I knew this moment—this night would come."

She threw back the blankets and slid over and onto him, tangling her toes around his ankles, slithering up and down his thighs, wriggling her belly all over him until he thought he would die or explode.

He grabbed for her, trying to reverse their positions, and she eluded his arms and knelt astride him, with her hands underneath to lift him to her. Even his very first time in the hayloft all those years ago, the blacksmith's expert and experienced daughter had not been so thoroughly in charge.

His face contorted, his body convulsed, and

197

he gasped out, "Amalie, oh God, Amalie, I'm sorry. You were so—I couldn't wait."

Hands tugged at his head, caught hold of his dark brown hair and wrenched it so fiercely that tears filled his eyes.

"Julianne," she hissed in his ear, as he lay inert, unable to move. "Julianne, not Amalie. Amalie is the pretty one and Julianne the plain. Amalie is dashing and Julianne is dull. Amalie gets all the attention and Julianne does the work."

Naked and avenging, Venus and vixen, she sat on his stomach and shook him furiously. "Listen to me, Alexander De Lacey, listen well. Not Amalie or Melrosa, only Julianne; but *I* am the one you are never going to forget. Don't worry about not having waited for me . . . we have a long night ahead, you and I."

She laughed deep in her throat. "When my sisters are just sweet fading memories, you will still be reliving this night. It will stay in your heart and mind forever, and so will I!"

Chapter Nineteen

England, 1784

The post office is a wonderful establishment . . . So seldom that a letter among the thousands . . . is ever carried wrong, and not one in a million, I suppose, actually lost!

—*Emma*
by Jane Austen

London
April 11th, 1784

Dear Cousin Frederick,

I have brought with me to town a letter of inquiry which I received from Mr. John Jay, written, he informed me, on your behalf.

By a most curious coincidence, it arrived

on the very day I departed Beaumont Hall for London, which was the first time I had left Derbyshire since my Original home-coming in January of 1781. My purpose in traveling up to London was to attend a Regimental Dinner this week, which will be my first time of Re-Union with many of the men I served with in America. They are but recently returned to England from our late Colonies, following the Treaty in Paris this past September, which officially ended the hostilities between your country and mine.

My dear Cousin, when I remember your many courtesies and kindnesses to me during my years in New York, I am covered with shame that you should have needed the services of an Attorney—even so acclaimed a one as Mr. Jay—to get account of me, and that I have never written other than the one brief note to inform you of my safe arrival home.

On the other hand, I promise you that I never received either of the two letters Mr. Jay implies were sent by you. Would that I had! I found myself suddenly so starved for news of you and those I cared for in America that the meagre information conveyed in his few paragraphs only whetted my appetite for more.

I learned from him that you married after the war ended and now spend your winters in Manhattan and your summers at Lacey Manor. Other than that—to my exasperation

—nothing. This one time, when I would gladly have welcomed a spate of words from a lawyer, the one employed in the business decided to be sparse with details.

Pray forgive me what may have seemed like indifference and neglect—but was far from being either—and write to me all that I would know. Until then I can only beg that you and your lady accept my heartiest felicitations and every wish for your present and future happiness.

The chased silver bowl with the family crest, which accompanies this letter, is a marriage gift from all your family here in England, and one we consider should rightly come to you, since it was bestowed on our common ancestor, in gratitude for his military services, by William, England's first Dutch King. Thus it seems entirely appropriate that it go now to the De Lacey branch which settled in the formerly Dutch colony of New York.

Now, as to my own life these three years and more since I returned home. Perhaps you will be more charitably inclined towards me—if indeed you were not so previously—when I explain the peculiar difficulties of my own situation.

As you know, I left America for England, uncertain as to whether my father and brother still lived. I arrived home to find both neither better nor worse than when I first received the news of Edward's accident.

The physicians assured me that only strength of will had kept my father alive till I returned; my mother was convinced that all he lived for was to see me wed to Lady Rona Falsorth before I inherited his Earldom of Beaumont.

Lady Rona and her father both being willing, the ceremony took place quietly in our family chapel within the week, with only the closest family members in attendance. There could naturally be no honeymoon journey at such a time, although I promised my wife we would travel to Paris at some future date.

From the day of my marriage, my amazing father, with a Resiliency the doctors could only marvel at, recovered apace. The Paralysis left his arms and more gradually his face and upper torso, so that the use of these parts of his body were little by little Restored and he recovered much of his speech. He cannot walk and is confined to an Invalid chair during whatever daytime hours he is not on the back of a horse. Our estate carpenter has created a special mounting block for him, a Marvel of simple engineering by which he is cranked up to the saddle in much the same manner that a small boat is lowered from the Mother Ship. Invalid or not, my father is very much a man, and now the doctors throw up their hands in disbelief and Affirm he will undoubtedly bury us all.

So, to my great gratitude, for I have ever

loved him dearly, I became not Earl of Beaumont.

Nor is it likely now that I ever will be, for something came to pass that Cousin Julianne spoke of my last night at Lacey Manor. When I unburdened myself of the dreadful news I had received, she said by way of comfort, "Perhaps it is not so dire as you fear. Miracles have happened." Even while I prayed for one, I was impatient with this remark because it struck me as the kind of sop one throws to a child.

Despite my lack of faith, a second miracle did happen, and Edward, after lying unconscious for slightly over a twelve-month, awoke one day as though he had but been to sleep the night before.

His memory was gone at first, but it returned to him, a little at a time, so that by the end of another year, his Brain was as active and intelligent as ever it had been. These last fourteen months he has been learning to walk again; and though it is a struggle, and he is often in pain, he has a strong Heart, and God knows, a brave one. He will never again walk completely upright or be entirely free from Physical suffering, but he should live out his full life span—at least, so I am assured.

My mother has lived through these Tribulations with remarkable fortitude, a tower of strength to my father and brother in their time of need, and indeed to me as well, for, in addition to supporting her in her endeavors, it was necessary all the past years for me to manage Beaumont and our other estates —work I was not bred to and at the time had no aptitude for. Indeed, I had to learn from my father's estate agent and his farmers, like the ignorant Scholar in such matters that I was.

Just lately my father and Edward have been able to do more, much more, and gradually they will be able to take the reins back into their own hands.

My father made over his house in London to me for the use of my wife, who prefers to spend the season in town, which my responsibilties to Beaumont and to my family did not previously permit.

We had a daughter born during our third year of marriage. She died at six weeks, which was a great grief to us.

All the above, dear Cousin, should make you reasonably au courant with my activities and give you almost as comprehensive a portrait of my present life as I have myself. Now, if you will, pray reciprocate. Describe your wife to me in the fullest detail so that I may see her presiding over the great round table in the dining hall, with the monteith bowl gleaming in the center. I want to be able to picture the two of you strolling along the long walk at Lacey Manor or crossing the wooden bridge over the duck pond.

I want to hear all that there is to hear of

*both you and yours, of all those who were
dear to you and, in days gone by, also to me.*

*Did Amalie ever return to New York, a
conquering heroine, since the Cause she
served prospered in the end?*

*And our dear little Melrosa . . . perhaps
not so little any longer. Did she ever make
the full recovery that all who loved her hoped
and prayed for?*

*Is Cousin Julianne still with you, or was
their own property ever restored to your
wards?*

They are ever in my thoughts, as are you.

> *Always, your Affectnte. Cousin,
> Alexander De Lacey*

Having subscribed his name to the end of
Frederick's letter, Alexander shook a stray
drop of ink from his quill into the ink pot, then
carefully laid his pen on the silver standish.

He leaned forward in his chair, with his
elbows propped on the handsome Hepple-
white desk recently purchased for the library
by his wife—no one, he thought, with a wry
twist of his lips, could fault her taste in furniture. His head fell forward into his hands,
and, as the arteries at his temples bulged and
the throbbing pain began, his fingertips began
an unconscious massaging motion across his
forehead.

When the hypnotic pressure of his hands
had eased away the worst pangs, he leaned

back in his chair, lifted the sheets of his letter and began to read it over. His eyes seemed to skim past certain phrases, while others fairly leaped out at him . . .

. . . my original homecoming in January of 1781. God! That nightmare journey! Pounding seas, incessant storms and waves the height of mountains: agonized weeks of seasickness, till he was convinced that even if the ship made port, *he* would not. Even worse, he had not cared. He seemed to be haunted equally by what he had left behind and what he might be going back to.

André, his friend, done to death by a hangman's noose, surely too horrible a price to pay for a combination of patriotism and ambition!

It was only MacDowell, patient, solid, persevering MacDowell, who had nursed him and lectured him and—much against his will at the time—forced him back to life.

Lady Rona and her father both being willing, the ceremony took place quietly . . .

Oh, so quietly and oh so quickly. Ah yes, *quickly,* that had been the key word. No more than her father, the impoverished Duke of Falsorth, did the well-bred, beautiful, respectable Lady Rona wish to let such a prize as the future Earl of Beaumont slip through her soft, slender, snow-white and—as he was to discover later—greedy and grasping fingers. She cared not whether her husband be Edward or

Alexander. The important thing was that *she* one day, hopefully quite soon, would be Countess of Beaumont.

There could naturally be no honeymoon journey at such a time ...

She was so much his notion, before he went to America, of what the perfect woman should look like—tall, regal, divinely fair of form and face—that all through the difficult first week home in England and even on their wedding day, he told himself over and over that it might turn out well. Presently he would forget about America, about *them*— about *her*. He and Lady Rona, working at it, could surely make the marriage a success.

The Lady Rona's maid was still there when he went to her room on their wedding night. His new wife wore a confection of pink lace and tulle that was any man's dream of how he would like to see his bride garbed when she welcomed him. She was pink-cheeked, pink-lipped, utterly lovely, even to the careful arrangement of golden curls cascading over her shoulders.

He walked towards her, trying to shut out the picture of Amalie in a torn nightdress and stained dressing gown, lifting a blotched, tear-stained face to his ... Julianne, naked and furious, sitting on his stomach and shaking him, shouting at him ...

"You may go, Mary," Lady Rona told her maid composedly, and stood waiting.

His hands were gentle on her shoulders. His kiss was light and utterly without passion. "My dear, I hope you are not frightened," he told her kindly.

"I do not frighten easily, sir," she told him in the same flat way she had spoken to the maid. "I admit to some slight—er—trepidation about the"—she made a little moue of distaste— "the ceremony we must engage in, but my mother assured me that I will soon grow accustomed, and I promise you that I will not shirk my duty, my Lord, either to Beaumont or to you. I know that you will want a son."

Bile rose in his throat. It was a moment before he could answer her. "My name is Alexander," he told her. "The sole title I can lay claim to—temporarily—is Major. Only my father is *my Lord* here."

"Oh, if you will split hairs, sir." Her smile was patronizing, her voice indulgent; she might have been a wise nanny dealing with her small, recalcitrant charge.

He wished with all his heart it was the mistress who had gone from the room and the maid remained. He could more easily appreciate bedding that buxom cheerful body than this cold empty statue of a woman who was already planning ahead to his father's and her former fiancé's death.

As he stood there, fighting rage and regret,

Lady Rona moved about the room, snuffing out the candles until only the one on the nightstand was left flickering. Then she removed the lacy gown and disposed herself gracefully on the bed, with the hem of her nightdress tucked modestly under her ankles. "I am ready, sir. You may come to me," she had invited him graciously.

The most desperate wish of his heart was to escape both the room and the house and never again set eyes on his wife of one day, but he knew his desire came too late. The freedom of choice was no longer his. They had made their bed, the Lady Rona and he, and they must both—God help them!—lie in it.

. . . My wife prefers to spend the season in town . . .

No cold statue any more but a boiling inferno of thwarted ambition! "You are crazed if you think I will spend another endless dull winter in this rural mausoleum with no one to dress for, no dinners or dances or anything that makes life worthwhile. You can do as you please, but I have no intention of wasting my life in the country with your saintly mother and your saintly self waiting for those two drooling cripples to die!"

. . . a daughter born during our third year of marriage . . .

"No, I don't want to see her!" Lady Rona had shrieked hysterically. "A daughter! What

209

good is a daughter to me? All those ghastly months and that horrible suffering to get a daughter. Now it all has to be gone through again."

"Not for *me!*" Alexander's icy voice was like a whiplash snapping across her hysteria. "Not ever again *with* me!"

"But we need a son for Beaumont."

"Beaumont will have its own sons. You have not spent enough time here of late to notice that Edward has fallen in love with Charlotte Phillips and she with him."

"Charlotte Phillips! You cannot mean the vicar's daughter, that dowdy, dowerless nobody! I don't believe it. Edward values himself too high; he would never stoop so low!"

"On the contrary, his illness and suffering have taught him humility and given him a true sense of values. Formerly he might not have had the wisdom and good taste to aspire to Charlotte instead of some witless society chit. Now, only his diffidence about his crippled state stands in the way of his asking for her, and Charlotte"—his face softened—"will take care of the proposal if Edward does not."

"But he's *deformed,*" she said with loathing.

"He is crippled, Madame," he corrected her, "and only in his legs. The part of him he needs for making sons is far from being impaired."

"You are vulgar and disgusting, sir."

"How strange, my Lady. I had much the same thought about you."

. . . describe your wife to me in the fullest detail . . .

Pray God, she is everything that mine is not, Cousin Frederick. Pray God, she makes you as happy as you deserve to be.

Did Amalie ever return to New York, a conquering heroine . . . ?

What matter since she returned not to him? Amalie, his beloved, his life; Amalie, who had wept wildly against his chest, kissed him sweetly as a child, lain innocently in his arms and pledged her love even while she practiced treachery. What had Julianne said on their last night? "I always knew she would betray you."

Oh, Amalie, Amalie, four years now, and I cannot forget you; four years, and how you haunt me still. How long will I, *must* I go on like this?

. . . Dear little Melrosa, perhaps not so little any more . . .

"London Bridge is falling down, falling down . . ." Sweet Melrosa, innocent Melrosa; suddenly, strangely sensuous Melrosa as she whirled about on the grass with gypsy abandon and a clutch of wildflowers in each of her hands.

* * *

. . . Is Cousin Julianne still with you?

How polite and stilted an inquiry, one that might properly be made of any passing acquaintance rather than of the passionate spinster with whom he had shared that long wild night of loving.

"I am the one you are never going to forget," she had told him. Told him truly. He remembered as though it were yesterday.

"This night will stay in your heart and mind forever," she had promised. A promise kept.

They are ever in my thoughts . . .

Ever. Always. Alexander laid down his letter and once more dropped his head against his hands. Was it true that he longed to be free of them? he wondered. Was it better to be haunted or bereft? Would he rather have the sweet bitterness of remembrance or life's emptiness if he forgot?

He did not know. He might never know.

Chapter Twenty

America to England, 1784-1788

How are the civilities and compliments of every day to
be related as they ought to be, unless noted down every
evening in a journal?

—*Northanger Abbey*
by Jane Austen

ENTRY IN THE ESTATE LEDGER OF LACEY
Manor, 9 June 1784

*Received from England this day a gift,
given in late acknowledgement of my marriage, by my distant kinsman Alexander De
Lacey and his family. It is a great silver bowl
with the family crest on one side, much
ornamented on the other with deeds of valor
that heralded the reign of William and Mary.
On the bottom side it is inscribed as being*

presented by King William to the first Lionel De Lacey.

At my dear wife's suggestion, I have given the bowl a prominent place on the table that stands just between the wall shelves in the library.

Extract from a letter to Alexander De Lacey written on the same day.

. . . You have deprived your own house of a precious heirloom to bestow it upon mine. My dear Cousin, although the generosity of your gift Fairley takes my Breath away, For two reasons, your choice was more Appropriate than you can conceive; the first being that my beloved wife is half of Dutch Extracktion, the second that my son is another Lionel. Lionel Frederick.

Lion—his Mother's name for him—is a fine, sturdy lad, for which I thank God every day of my life. I sorrow at the Death of your daughter. It is almost two Decades since I lost the child of my first Marriage, but as we both know Now, it is a Pain that may be softened by Time but never entirely leaves one.

Describe my wife, you asked me . . . Need I? Have you not, perhaps, alreddy Guessed? The very week after you left America, Julianne suddenly desided to Journey to Jersey. She had my Heartiest Blessing because the purpose of her Going was to make her

Peace with Amalie. A few days after Julianne's leaving, Melrosa came Home to Lacey Manor, as Lovely and Blooming a girl as she had been before the Fire of '76. Amalie returned to the Theatre and joined a Traveling Company. Julianne, surprizingly, went with her, not to Act, but to more or less Manage and House-Keep for the Company. She wrote me that her life had Hithertoo been too Circumscribed and she craved a little Adventure. They both urged Melrosa to join them, but Melrosa told me that Lacey Manor was her home and she would never leave it, except by Will of mine. This Declaration gave me the Courage to make one of my own. In that case, I told her, she would never leave, not during her Life-Time or Mine.

We were sitting at BreakFast when this conversation took place, and her eyes met mine across the table in a look that will be with me as long as I draw Breath. She gave me a Smile of incredibill Sweetness and a look so full of love and trust that the swelling of my heart seemed to fill up all my body. Then she reached out both Hands to me, and I put my plain signet ring on her finger. (She has never allowed me to replace it with a jeweled one.) The first Banns were read in Church the next day.

I am nearing the Half-Century mark of my Life, a time when many men begin to think of a Rocking Chair by the fire and a Cure for their gout. Yet here I am the posessor of such Happiness as I never thought Possible for a Young Man, let alone an Old.

My littel French Rose is no longer a frightened Child needing Protection. She has grown in Beauty, Strenth, and Wisdom. She is a lovely Serene Presence, Sunshine and Laffter filling my House as I think you long ago may have Suspeckted she filled my Heart . . .

Entry in the Estate Ledger of Lacey Manor, 4 April 1785

The English newspapers I received from my agent in Manhattan contained the news of the death of Alexander's father, Lionel, Earl of Beaumont. I at once Penned my Condolenses to Alex and my Wife wrote seperettely to the Dowager Countess. Alexander will be sore Grieved, I know. I dowt it will afford him much Consolation that his father's last five years were really a Gift from Heaven.

Entry in the Estate Ledger of Lacey Manor, 22 September 1785

An order placed this day with Jos. Barnes, silversmith, for a set of painted pewter soldiers representing the Fifth Regiment of Foot, the Regiment originally formed in Holland, which served in America during the late Hostilities: to be sent as a Christening gift for Henry Richard, the new little heir to Edward De Lacey, Earl of Beaumont.

I had thought the Implications of such a gift might Offend (they did lose the War), but my Wife pointed out that the Beaumonts hardly had need of another silver mug sent all the way from America . . . British soldiers could not offend British Nobility . . . and the Child himself would get much Pleasure in the future from Such a Gift.

Extract from letter to Alexander De Lacey written on the same day

. . . 'Tis true, I was not surprized by your news. It Appeared to me that all your last letters hinted at such a Step, and your father's and brother's joynt Generossity made it Possibel.

Although I Acknowledge that a younger son is seldom the Possessor of such a Valuable Estate and the Fortune to maintain it, I am also in accord with their Sentiment that, for your Years of Unselfish Devotion and Sacrifice, you more than Deserve all that has been given you.

With your father dead and your mother Established in the Dower House at Beaumont, it seems as right and proper that you have a home, a place of your Own, as that your brother and his Littel Family begin their own life of Independency.

Perhaps your Wife may now be willing to

live in Sussex with you and there will be another Child. . . .

Entry in the Estate Ledger of Lacey Manor, 17 August, 1786

Our last gift of this nature, having provided such obvious Pleasure, an order placed with Jos. Barnes, Silversmith, for a set of painted pewter soldiers of a British Grenadier Company: a christening gift for Lionel Jonathan, second son of the Earl of Beaumont.

Extract from letter to Alexander De Lacey written the following day:

. . . Your letter from London reached me here, after some Delay, the Direction having been Mis-Writen, probably in your Distress.
I am sorely Grieved for you that your wife's first stay in Sussex is Caused by such a Serious Illness, but perhaps the change from the City Life, as well as the Country Air, may be of benefit to Lady Rona. Perhaps, also, to your Relationship . . .

Entry in the Estate Ledger of Lacey Manor, 10 July 1787

An order placed with Jos. Barnes, Silver-smith, for a set of painted pewter soldiers of Queen's Own Regiment of Light Dragoons as

*christening gift for William Jeremy, third
son of the Earl of Beaumont.*

*Mr. Barnes, a sober man but evidently not
without Humour, suggested I make a permanent yearly Order, which suggestion may be
Timely with my cousin, Edward De Lacey
and his good wife, seemingly so set on popu-
lating Britain with little male Beaumonts.*

If only Alexander . . .

**Extract from letter to Alexander De Lacey
written a week later**

*. . . The Cycle of Life is invariabel, as we
Farmers know only too well. Fast on the heels
of your Nefhew's Birth came the word of the
Death of your Wife, the Lady Rona. I know
not what to say to you, dear Cousin, who
have known so much of sorrow these last
Years . . .*

**Entry in the Estate Ledger of Lacey Manor,
3 September 1787**

*The two doctors have just left, their Con-
sultation carefully timed for my Wife's visit
with our son to West Chester. I will not have
a Physician here again—not till it be necessary. There is no need. I know what is Ahead
and I know what I must do. All that matters
to me now is ensuring the Wellfare and Happiness of the two who are dearer, far dearer,
than my Life to me.*

Melrosa, Beloved Wife, some time after I am gone, when you are in Charge, you may probably come to read the Paragraph above and be Angry with me for not taking you Immediately into my Confidense. Forgive me, my love, and try to understand that in my Mans Vanity I wanted to be that many months longers the one at the Helm you looked to. All too soon it may be the other way round . . .

My son, you may read these words one day, and perhaps you will better understand. I Grieve that I cannot live to see you Full-Grown.

From MacDowell to Mr. De Lacey in December 1787 (found many years later in binding of estate ledger)

Dear Sir, Yrs. recvd. and I am most happy to anser tho the anser is not happy just as the Major isnt. As long as we was at Beaumont it wasnt too bad becus he had a gole to work for helping his father and brother, and it dint mater so much abowt his wife. Preechers say not to speak ill of the dead but I spok just as ill when she was alive and its Gods truwth she never forgave him becus he dint becom the Earl and she made his life Hell and evryone at Beaumonts life Hell to. They gave her the London house and plenty money to stay in it to get rid of her. The Major was good to her. I cant get over his pashense because I got to admit hes not a pashent man but I understud when he sed one day that he dint have anything else to give her so he owed her that. He dint mean money, he ment himself. He only turned agenst her when she took on abowt having the girl insted of a son and dint even greeve when the poor thing died. Still when she got sick herself it wasnt her hi-nose family took care of her, it was the Major. She took nearly a year dying and he was mitey good to her wich wasnt eazy becus her dying was prity awfull. It came abowt becus after she got well of the Chikenpox she put so much cozmeticks on her face to cover the spots, she was that prowd of her looks, and they say it was the cozmeticks gave her the led poizoning sickness. Anyhow now he puts all his time and feerce ennergey to take grate care of Tipperley, wich is the name of the estayt but I dont think he truwly likes Sussex. He workds hard all day and sits alone at nite reading and riting, axcept a coupel of times a week he and I play cards and drink and talk, and the talk is mostly abowt the Army and America. Every three or fore months he goes away himself for a week and cums back looking like deth and I no what hes been up to, wel hes no monk, and then he goes on like befor. Is this what you wanted to here sir? I wish it cud be beter news. Respectfully yrs. MacDowell.

FRENCH ROSE

De Lacey House
Great George Street
New York
5 January 1788

My dear Alexander,

I have come into the City for a week, primarily to Conduct some affairs of Business. Melrosa is with me, but we left Lion with our HouseKeeper at Lacey Manor because, contrary to our Usual Custom, we have desided to spend the entire Winter there this year. One of our prezent Pre-Ocupations is to choose a tutor to take back with us for our son, so that (much to his Consturnation) his Schooling will not be intirrupted. We are to intervue a young man from the College of Yale this very afternoon, which is why I feel Urgent to finish this letter, there is so much I wish to say to you.

In September of last year a Suspision of my own was Confirmed to me by physicians, which is that I have not a great Time longer to live. This is not the odd case of your father, even of your brother, my dear Cousin. There was no Accident, no Seezure, just the slow and Unfortunettely sure Progress of a Diseaze from which there can be no Recovery.

I do not cumplain of my Ill Fortune. I have no right to, having been given late in life

such Happiness as few men ever know. I
have had more than seven Years with Melrosa. True, I would like doubel, trebel that
time—what Man is not Greedy?—but there
are Reasons for all things, and I am Ready, I
hope, when the Time comes, to Axcept the
bad as I have the good.

My affairs are in order. Lacey Manor is for
Melrosa; my larger Estate in Yonkers and its
lands are a goodly Inheritance for my son.
There are monies in plenty for him too. Melrosa has a Settelment which will keep her
in life's Comforts as well as Elegansies for
all her life, and this house on Great George
Street is also hers. She never wanted the
one on Broad Way, used by the Army, because
of her bad Memories, so I sold it after the
War.

But we have lived so much to ourselves,
the boy, she and I, and she has no family left.
(Since Amalie and Julianne married and
went west, it is not Likely now that they will
ever Return.) I worry about Melrosa left
alone, a beautiful woman not yet thirty. And
Lion . . . a boy needs a man to look to, a
Model for his own Deportment.

Cousin, I would not dream of asking you to
give up your Life in England, but if after I
am gone, you were willing to spend a few
months in New York every other few years, I
would—with your Consent—join you in the
Gardianship of my son, Melrosa, of course, to

223

have the final say in all matters relating to his upbringing, and also my lands.

I would not dream of making such a Reqwest if you had a Wife and Family of your own, or if you should be thinking of ack-wiring these firm Anchors to ones own Harth and Home.

If, however, you are not; and if you still have the same Urge for Wandering and Adventure I sensed in you when you were here in America . . .

I would that—if you Consider my Propozal —you think about it carefully and at Lenth. I want no hasty Acceptence made out of Sentiment. This propozal must Serve your Interests as well as my Own. If you do not feel you could leave England for such long Periods, there is no more to be said; and Beleeve me when I say I will understand, for had this same Propozal ever been put to me, I must have Unhezitatingly Refused. Nothing could have Indused me to leave Melrosa and my son for months at a time.

If, however, you are of a mind to say yes, then I will at Once make Arrangements with my Attorney and Friend, Mr. John Jay, who allreddy knows of my Predickament.

My dear Cousin, one of my life's grate pleasures, after my Wife and Son, has been the close Bond that came to exist between us.

Your Affectnte. Cousin,
Frederick De Lacey

New York
20 April 1788

My dear Mr. De Lacey:

As his attorney, it is my sad duty to acquaint you with the news of the death of your cousin, Mr. Frederick De Lacey, which sad event occurred exactly one week ago. He was laid to rest in the family cemetery, which lies just behind the wilderness at Lacey Manor, Turtle Bay.

I think it will ease your grief to know that shortly before the end—which came on quickly after he took a suddenly unexpected turn for the worse—he had received your letter written in March. He was made very happy by the news it conveyed, to wit: your willingness to be joined in the guardianship of his son and the care of the estate and to spend much of your time in America until young Lionel is old enough to manage his own properties.

An addition was immediately made to his will, along with the usual safeguards. He asked me to transmit by letter this one last request, which is that you not come to America until his dear wife's year of mourning is over. Knowing her nature, he considered her more capable of dealing alone with the initial period of sorrow she and her son are bound to experience before she comes to terms with her changed life.

At the same time, he felt this period of

preparation would give you the opportunity to arrange your own affairs without undue precipitation.

I will be most happy to assist you in any way possible. Along with my condolences, I should like to offer you the assurance that Mr. De Lacey had the greatest faith in your loyalty to his dear family and good judgement regarding their needs.

Respectfully Yrs.,
John Jay, Attoreny

Entry in the Estate Ledger of Lacey Manor, 2 October 1788

As I know would have been my dear husband's wish, I placed an order with Jos. Barnes, Silversmith, for a set of painted pewter soldiers of Fraser's Highlanders, to be sent to England as a christening gift for Edward James, fourth son of the Earl and Countess of Beaumont.

Chapter Twenty-one

New York, February 1789

Old England is our home, and English-
men are we;
our tongue is known in every clime,
our flag in every sea.

—Mary Howitt

ON A WET WINDY DAY IN MID-FEBRUARY OF
1789, without any of the unwelcome fuss and
fanfare that had distinguished their leaving,
Alexander De Lacey and MacDowell landed
in the city they had departed more than eight
years before.

Since they were seven or eight weeks ahead
of their scheduled arrival, MacDowell stayed
at the ship to supervise the unloading and

stowing onto a carrier's wagon of a huge quantity of luggage. De Lacey hired a carriage to take him to John Jay's office.

Mr. Jay, though expressing great delight to meet the gentleman from England with whom he had been in close correspondence for some nine months, was a little concerned about this change in plans. The house on Cherry Street, for which he had arranged a year's rental on behalf of his client's cousin, would not be ready for occupancy for another ten days, possibly a fortnight. The housekeeper he had hired for Mr. De Lacey did not plan to be in residence till the first of March. As for the carriage ordered from William Collett on Wall Street—he was sorry to say that, due to the exorbitant salary demands of the coachmaker's laborers, it seemed unlikely to be finished much before spring.

With a reasonableness Mr. Jay had evidently not expected from even a younger branch of the British aristocracy, Alexander made soothing sounds and suggestions.

He and his man could stay at one of the taverns—City, perhaps, or Fraunces—until house and housekeeper were ready. As for the carriage, it was of no great moment that it was unfinished. He did not plan any immediate travel and, for the present, could use hired hacks about the city.

Mr. Jay, charmed by this tact and agreeableness, ventured a suggestion of his own. If he might presume—the taverns were noisy, bustling places; Mr. De Lacey might be more comfortable at Mrs. Daubigny's boarding house on Wall Street, quite near to the coach-maker's and the center of fashionable life and business.

When Alex concurred, the lawyer dispatched his young secretary Remsen to the dock to direct MacDowell to Mrs. Daubigny's. In all courtesy Alex then invited Mr. Jay to lunch with him, though he had seldom so begrudged the giving of two hours.

Even as he and the attorney drank their Madeira and discussed the changing face of New York since the British evacuation, he smiled ruefully to himself at his own frenzied restlessness. Eight years and half as many months since he had set eyes on Frederick's little French Rose, and suddenly two hours were an eternity.

Even an eternity ends. At three o'clock, with his heart beating as erratically as a schoolboy's summoned to the headmaster's study, he was lifting the knocker of the fashionable brick house on Great George Street.

There was instant recognition on both sides when a maid in a somber gray gown and white apron answered the door. Plump, middle-aged Dutch Mary had not altered noticeably since the day he apologized to her at Lacey Manor for the gaucherie of offering her coin for service.

"Major De Lacey," she said, with a broad,

bright smile as she gestured him in and reached for his hat. "Welcome home, sir."

Home? A sudden mist dimmed his eyes. England was home. In England were the graves of his father, his wife, his daughter. In England were his mother, his brother, his family, Beaumont, his own estate.

Home? "Thank you, Mary," he said huskily, "but it's not Major any longer. I sold out of the army eight years ago."

"Just as well, sir," she remarked placidly. "It's live and let live here in New York since the peace came, but the uniform is still not too popular."

"Is Mel—Mrs. De Lacey at home?"

"She's in the library. Would you like to wait in the parlor, sir, while I fetch her?"

"I would rather surprise her in the library if you will please show me the way."

She hesitated just a moment; then the same cheerful smile beamed his way again. "I daresay this one time she would like to be surprised," she decided tolerantly. "Come along, sir."

He went along, meekly, and when she stopped and pointed with one finger, he quietly turned the knob of the door indicated and walked inside.

Two walls of the library were lined with well-stacked bookshelves. There was a healthy fire blazing in the fireplace and extra warmth coming from an ugly pot-bellied Franklin stove at the far end of the room.

Near to the stove was a handsome, mahogany desk, with a slender figure sitting at it, her back to him. She was bending over what looked like an accounting ledger.

"Tea time already, Mary?" She yawned and stretched but did not turn around. "I don't know where the hours went. I'll come over to the table in a moment. Isn't Lion home from school yet?"

She never heard the silent footsteps across the old Oriental carpet, its blues and scarlets so faded to dull olive it was no longer considered a suitable wall decoration.

When his hand lightly touched her shoulder, she looked up, startled, and a little cry escaped her lips. "Alexander!" Then she said it again, this time in a whisper. "Alexander."

Suddenly her face, which had gone dead white, seemed to spring into life again. The color came back to her cheeks and the radiance to her eyes. She jumped up from her chair and put both hands against the front of his jacket. "Alexander," she said a third time, a sob sounding in her voice. "Welcome, welcome back."

"Mary said, 'Welcome home,' my dear. That sounded even better."

"Then welcome home, dear Cousin." This time it was her face she pressed against his chest, drawing a deep, quivering sigh as his arms slipped lightly about her.

When she raised her head and retreated a little, they stood staring at each other, their minds both busy with thoughts of the distance and living and years that had come between.

"My God, you look like Amalie!" he said presently.

She gave him a smile of childish mischief that was like the Melrosa of old.

"Surely not as beautiful as *that!*" she teased him.

He studied the oval face, the smooth skin, the golden hair that used to swing behind her like a banner but was now swept sedately up to the top of her head in a handsome coronet of braids.

"Every bit as beautiful," he said so quietly that she gave him a quick, sharp look, then shook her head in self-castigation.

"I'm sorry, Alexander," she apologized. "Does it—does it still hurt remembering her?"

"No, of course not. It's been a long time."

She raised one skeptical eyebrow, a comical look of disbelief on her face. He had to laugh. "Ah, well, an occasional twinge or two now and then," he admitted.

She came close to him and stood on tiptoe to peer up into his face. He had forgotten what a little thing she was. He looked down, and this time his shout of laughter was genuinely amused. White-stockinged feet peeped out from underneath the pale lavender under-skirt of her gown. Her shoes, black leather with big silver buckles, stood neatly side by side next to the desk.

They were sensible square-toed Dutch shoes of the kind Julianne used to wear. For a moment his heart ached wih a fleeting memory of the dainty dancing slippers that had served Amalie on every occasion.

"Oh, my dear." Melrosa touched her hand briefly to one of his cheeks. "Has it been that bad? You look so—so—.You look older." She began to sniff, and he started reaching for his handkerchief. If she was the same Melrosa, she would not have her own.

"I *am* older."

"I know, but—but it *shows!*" she burst out.

"My dear girl." His lips twisted wryly as he handed over his handkerchief. "Did Cousin Frederick never teach you to cultivate some tact? Men are no different than women in disliking to be told that they look older. Your Mary was much more flattering; she gave me the impression I had not altered a bit."

Melrosa blew her nose vigorously, then used the edges of his handkerchief to mop delicately at her eyes. "I didn't m-mean you l-looked old," she said, more tears falling. "I meant you l-looked as though—you—you h-had a b-bad time. D-did you?"

His first impulse was to turn away her question with a smile and a jest. Disarmed by her candor and touched by her tears, he substituted honesty. "Yes, Melrosa," he told her. "I had a bad time."

"I'm so sorry." She continued her soft weeping until the handkerchief was reduced to a sodden rag. Sighing, he handed over his spare.

"Were *you* happy, Melrosa?"

"*I* had—I have my son. He is the most wonderful boy in the world, Alexander," she assured him earnestly. "He's sunny and sweet-tempered and smart, maybe a little more solemn this last year, but then, he does miss Frederick so."

Under his unblinking stare, she laughed a little nervously. "He is much more a De Lacey than a van Raalte, I can tell you, except that his hair is the color and texture of corn silk, fine and golden, just like mine when I was his age."

"I asked if *you* were happy, Melrosa."

"Frederick *made* me happy. He was the most wonderful husband a woman could have. I'm growing accustomed, but at times I do miss him unbearably," she choked out. "And you—your wife—?"

"Tell me about Amalie and Julianne," he interrupted firmly.

"Oh, dear, of course." She looked at him from under her lashes, trying to judge how much her answer meant to him. "Well, there isn't much to tell; it's been a long time since I got direct word of them. They married in Virginia—planters, two brothers—and they somehow all decided to go west. Ohio . . . Kentucky . . . I'm not sure where they finally arrived, or even"—she swallowed—"*if they* arrived, there are so many dangers on the way. I may never know. They may as well have gone to another continent. They are out of my life forever."

"I'm sorry, Melrosa. I didn't mean to make you sad."

There was a constriction across his chest that astonished and enraged him. These last few years, with the pain diminished and the memories no longer an ever-present torment, he had been able to tell himself that the yearnings of the past were over. Had he been fooling himself all this while? Had he crossed an ocean after eight long years in futile and secret hope of rekindling the past? If so—he smiled grimly to himself—the more fool he.

He turned towards Melrosa, a change of subject ready on his lips, when the door of the library was flung open and an older, yellow-haired version of his brother's second son came bursting into the room.

"Mama, I got all my 'rithmetick questions perfect, can I have two cakes for tea? I'm starving. I'm the starvingest I've ever been."

"Lion, your manners! We have a guest. This is your Cousin Alexander just arrived from England."

The boy snatched off his tricorn and held it across his stomach, bowing stiffly. "I am pleased to meet you, Cousin Alexander," he said formally. Then, quickly reverting to the child, "Were you the one who was our enemy in the war, sir?"

"I was a British soldier, Lionel, but I was never your enemy. Your father was my dear friend."

"I thought you and my Dad was cousins."

"We were cousins and friends, as I hope you and I will be."

The boy looked an inquiry at his mother. When she nodded, smiling, he began to smile too.

"I will be your cousin *and* friend, sir, and you may call me Lion like my other friends do," he invited graciously.

"Thank you, Lion."

After the two shook hands gravely, Melrosa told her son, "Go wash your hands, Lion, and tell Mary we will have our tea in the parlor. Yes," she forestalled him, "you may have two cakes."

As he erupted out of the room with enough noise to simulate a cavalry charge, Alexander grinned across at her. "A very cowed and disciplined child, I see."

"He *is* disciplined when he needs it," Melrosa retorted defensively. "He's a good boy." She thought a minute. "Most of the time," she added scrupulously; then "I hope Mr. Jay told you that, even if you are part-guardian, *I* have the final say about his—"

"Hey!" He came close and shook her gently. "I was but teasing. Your Lion is a fine sturdy boy with good manners and plenty of proper spirit, everything you and his father claimed. You are right, too, about his being every inch a De Lacey. I have seen that face in at least a dozen of the family portraits at Beaumont." Another light shake. "So you may sheathe your claws, mother tigress. They are not needed in defense of your young. *Or* to remind me of the limits of my authority."

She smiled, blushed, then wriggled free of his hold.

"I'm sorry," she said, her voice subdued. "It's not that you . . . I *am* grateful to you . . . It's just that he's all I have."

"Not any longer."

She looked away. "I wanted to write to you to tell you not to feel obliged to come here from England, but Mr. Jay told me I should not. He said you were a man of honor, and you had written him that you had a promise to keep. I know you did it for Frederick's peace of mind, and I am—I am—" She gulped, trying to get the words out. He was reminded not so much of Amalie as of the little girl who had run from him in the garden. "I am grateful," she went on resolutely, "but you are not to feel bound by that promise for more than—more than a reasonable visit."

"Are you inviting me to leave when I have but just arrived?"

"No, of course not, I just want you to understand that you need not make any sacrifices on our account."

"I am not the sacrificing sort."

"But you promised Frederick."

"Because I wanted to."

She stared at him, wide-eyed. "I don't understand."

"It is eight years, three months, and I-don't-know-how-many-days since I left New York for England. In all that time I have never really felt alive."

"But you were often unhappy here!"

"True. But at times I was also wildly happy, and looking back now, the one was worth the other. I meant what I told Lion. Frederick was both my cousin and my friend, but I'm not here just because he wanted me to be. I wanted to come, Melrosa. I believe I may be in search of something that went out of my life after I left America."

"You can't mean Amalie or Julianne," she protested. "You knew they were both married. Anyhow, you didn't even like Julianne. It was Amalie you were madly in love with. I was just the little mad sister, the one you felt sorry for."

"Not any longer, Melrosa," he said again.

"I beg your pardon."

"Have you glanced in your looking glass lately, Melrosa? Believe me, I don't feel sorry for you. No one could. I feel sorry for myself."

Her eyes opened wider and wider. "Cou-sin Al-exander," she faltered.

"Alex," he corrected. "Just plain Alex, Melrosa."

The door burst open again. "Mama, where are you? Mary says the tea is ready, and I washed my hands shining clean. There are extra cakes for Cousin Alexander too."

"Cousin Alexander is grateful," said that gentleman, lifting the child onto his shoulder. With the boy bouncing triumphantly up and down, he proceeded to the parlor.

Melrosa followed meekly, a hand on each of her burning cheeks.

Chapter Twenty-two

New York, February 1789

"The allurements of New York are more than 10 to 2
compared with Philadelphia."

—*Diary of Senator Maclay of Pennsylvania, 1780's*

"BOARDING HOUSE, INDEED! YOU'LL DO NO
such thing. This is New York, not England,"
Melrosa admonished him with energy. "I'll
fetch my writing desk so you can write a
note to MacDowell, and my man Jemmie
will take it right down to the dock. If he's already left for Mrs. Daubigny's—"

Alexander put up both hands to stem the
tide of her eloquence.

"Mr. Jay agreed with me; it's not a question
of hospitality but of propriety."

He laughed as she stared at him in affront. "My house is crawling with servants," she reminded him scornfully.

"Now don't eat me, but Mr. Jay is in the right of it. You are a young and very beautiful widow while I am a not-as-young but nevertheless eligible widower. We mustn't provide any fuel for the gossips."

She lifted her brows in derision, and he added coaxingly, "Not that either of us care, but for Lion's sake."

He was startled to see all the color drain from her face. For a minute she seemed unable to speak. Then, "As you wish," came from between her pinched lips. "For Lion's sake."

"What did I say, Melrosa?"

"I beg your pardon."

"What did I say to upset you so?"

"Nothing. Nothing."

"Now that," he observed conversationally, with a quick glance to make sure that Lion was too absorbed in selecting extra cake to be listening, "is one great lie."

Melrosa said haughtily, "You haven't changed a bit, after all, Major. You're as arrogant as you ever were."

"And you, my dear," he returned amiably, "are become just as imperious as Amalie and almost as pugnacious as Julianne. Whatever happened to sweet Melrosa?"

There was a pregnant pause, with their future good relations very much at stake.

241

Then suddenly the two of them burst out laughing.

"Sweet Melrosa grew up," she was finally able to control her voice sufficiently to say, "she grew up and out of her sweetness."

"She certainly did," Alex agreed cordially, at which she wrinkled her nose at him.

"Mama." Having finally eaten his full, Lion was at her side, tugging at her sleeve. "Why for are you and my new cousin laughing so loud?"

"Because we're happy, darling. That's why people laugh."

"We're happy to be together, Lion," Alex explained, gently drawing the boy between his knees. "People who love each other like to be together."

Lion nodded, satisfied, and Melrosa lowered her hot face into her tea cup.

"I think," Alexander said reluctantly, setting down his own cup, "I had better get over to Mrs. Daubigny's."

"May I come with you?" Melrosa asked impulsively. "It's so long since I've seen Mac-Dowell. Has he changed much?"

"Half a stone heavier but otherwise just the same. Come to think of it, I don't know why I should take especial note of *your* belligerence. I should be too accustomed to it from my own household. He rules me, as always, with a rod of iron."

"Mama, may I come too?" Lion was prancing up and down in his eagerness. "I want to see Sir MacDowell."

Alexander looked at mother and son, his eyebrows and voice both raised. "*Sir* Mac-Dowell?"

"Oh, yes!" Lion chirped enthusiastically. "He was just like King Arthur's knights riding to the rescue of the fair young maiden. Mama said he risked life and limb and—and I forget the other thing, but he risked everything to ride to the Manor and give warning that the British were on the way, just like a noble knight would. So that makes him *Sir*, and I want to see him—please, Mama, please take me with you."

"If you promise to do all your lessons before bed." He nodded in solemn ecstasy. "Then tell Jemmie to have the carriage sent round and get yourself a warm cape."

As he went rushing out, Alexander turned to give Melrosa a silent, searching look. "Does the boy know his Aunt Amalie was a spy for the American side?" he queried softly.

Melrosa's cup clattered in her saucer. She spoke even more softly. "That is a word we never use in this house. You must remember" —she smiled tentatively—"Lion is of the first generation that describes itself solely as American, not English."

"But his father was—"

"Once the war was over and there was no turning back, his father became completely dedicated to the independent United States," Melrosa cut in eagerly.

"Mr. Jay was quite cordial to me," he said slowly, "but he, of course, as well as being an attorney, is a diplomat. Will my past as a British officer make me unwelcome here in New York, do you think? And will it—I would not want to make difficulties for you with your neighbors."

Melrosa laid her hand on his sleeve and smiled in reassurance. "During the British occupation, New York was honeycombed with Patriots—like Amalie—who concealed their true bent. Now the reverse is true. There were so many Tories left when you British decamped, we had no choice—except in the most outrageously partisan cases—but to accept them. We live side by side now, Patriot and Tory, in what is sometimes uneasy amity, but amity nevertheless. It may not be true in England—I am sure it is not—but here we respect and mourn John André as sincerely as we do Nathan Hale."

"Your countrymen are more generous than mine, then." He got up and took a restless turn or two about the room. "Poor André. I paid my respects to his mother and sisters as soon as I could after I reached England; I don't recall ever doing anything more difficult. They adored him and were devastated by his death, particularly the mode of it."

"He was a loving son and a most devoted brother," Melrosa agreed compassionately. "I remember how anxious he was to succeed for their sake as well as for his own."

Alexander looked down at her in surprise. "I didn't know that you were acquainted with André."

Melrosa set her tea cup on the serving tray and carefully brushed some crumbs from the lap of her dress.

"Did you not?" she asked casually. "He used occasionally to come to Lacey Manor with Sir Henry; perhaps it was before you arrived in America. He was always very kind to me."

Mary appeared in the open doorway. "Mrs. De Lacey, ma'am." Her eyes were bright and her blown cheeks red with indignation. "There's an uppish creature at the door claims to be—he says—the Major's man."

Alexander grinned. "I believe," he murmured, "that Lion is about to meet *Sir* Mac-Dowell. If you will excuse me a moment, Melrosa . . ."

She waited expectantly for him to return, which he did in just a few minutes, laughing and rueful.

"If MacDowell and I might trespass on your hospitality for a few days—your city seems to be filling up with politicians and business men, and Mrs. Daubigny has no free rooms at present."

"I have a good mind to make you go to one of the taverns," Melrosa said severely. "What about the proprieties? What about my fragile widow's reputation?"

"I'm defeated, rolled up. I surrender."

"Where is MacDowell?"

"With Mary in the kitchen getting a bite to eat. I suspect it will be war to the teeth between them."

"Tell Lion."

Melrosa picked up her skirts to run, remembered her shoes, returned to slip them on, then skittered out of the room as though she were not much older than her son. When Alexander and Lion arrived in the kitchen a little later, she sat beside MacDowell at the work table, talking eagerly, while he worked his way through a man-sized platter of food, the most benign smile Alex ever remembered seeing lighting up his face.

"MacDowell, this is my son, Lionel Frederick De Lacey. Lion, this is the gentleman who rode like a gallant knight to save m-my—your aunt."

MacDowell's complexion became a rich dark ruby. "Such stuff to be filling your son's head with!" he scolded Melrosa. "You, boy, there was no saving to be done. The lady had already rescued herself."

Lion's face fell woefully. "But Sir MacDowell—"

"Just plain MacDowell will do," growled the knight in question. "If it's heroics you're wanting, how about the lady herself? A finer one there never lived than her."

"But ladies can't be knights."

"Who said so?"

"They have to sit in their castles waiting to be rescued from the dragons."

"Rubbish!" snorted MacDowell with a mighty roll of his *r*'s. "As often as not, it's the other way around. Ladyships can be knights and heroes too. The Lady Amalie"—he gave Melrosa a swift, piercing glance that sent waves of shock racing through her body— "was the bravest knight I ever knew."

"Mary," she said hastily, "will you show Mr. De Lacey to his room—the master's suite. Lion may stay here. I'll see you later, MacDowell."

Then she swooped down for a moment, and Alexander De Lacey smiled inwardly to himself, trying to fancy his late wife, or any English lady he knew, pressing her aristocratic cheek, even for a second, to the stubbled one of her husband's batman.

That night, sitting by the fire in a maple rocker, in the room that had been Frederick De Lacey's, he was smiling over the second volume of *Tom Jones* when a light knock sounded on the door.

"Come in," he called, thinking it was MacDowell.

Engrossed in his book, he did not look up till the door closed, and his nostrils began twitching from a familiar haunting aroma.

Hot mulled cider.

He felt strangely removed from the present,

almost as though he had been hurled back in time. A girl—no, a woman in a flowing, flowered gown was offering him a steaming mug.

The memories came flooding back, wonderful and painful. The mind pictures were pressing down on his brain; it was suddenly hard to breathe.

"Julianne," he muttered, her aphrodisiac apple fragrance reminding him of the taste of those incredible kisses. Then he closed his eyes and added, "Amalie," for the apparition had the look, the grace of that other sister, the spy who had loved and betrayed him.

"It's Melrosa," said a quiet, controlled voice. "I remembered at Lacey Manor you used to like a drink of hot cider before you slept. No, don't get up."

She came swiftly over to the rocker, bent and offered the mug to him again. He took it automatically.

"Good night, Alexander," she said softly.

She was almost at the door before he answered. "Good night, Melrosa."

He stood up and moved away from the fire after she left, the sweat pouring down his face and all over his body. He threw *Tom Jones* onto the rocker and yanked off his dressing gown.

It had taken every ounce of strength, all the will he possessed not to grab her and toss her onto the bed . . . use her to get rid of the aching memories. He felt suddenly convinced that only by making mad wild love to their little sister could he exorcise the haunting spirits of Amalie and Julianne.

"Oh, Christ, I must be going mad!" he said aloud.

The scent of cinnamon and apples was everywhere in the room; so was a vision of the exquisitely-formed pocket Venus who had walked across to him, perfectly, proudly naked. As though it were just last night, he could remember the golden sheen of her skin, the two thick braids tied with silver ribbons.

He groaned aloud, feeling his loins contract. Tears of frustration mingled with his sweat. Just when he thought he had forgotten, it all came flooding back . . . the sweat and salt tears and sweet cider mingling in their kisses . . .

"When my sisters are just sweet fading memories, you will still be reliving this night. It will stay in your heart and mind forever, and so will I!"

Chapter Twenty-three

New York, March-April, 1789

That I should love a bright particular star
And think to wed it.

—*All's Well That Ends Well*
William Shakespeare

THE FEW DAYS' HOSPITALITY DE LACEY HAD asked for stretched into ten before he and MacDowell, the new housekeeper hired by Mr. Jay, and an assortment of housemaids acquired through Mr. Cavenaugh's "Intelligence Office," moved into the house on Cherry Street, rightly advertised as "in genteel surroundings, with spacious gardens, eight fireplaces, generous sized chambers, and stabling for a gentleman's carriage and four horses."

It was not seemly for Melrosa to visit his bachelor quarters, though she and Lion came there to Sunday supper with Mr. and Mrs. Jay, but for the next several weeks Alexander dined at the house on Great George Street almost as often as when he was in residence there. Toward the end of March, he used his newly finished carriage for a journey through West Chester.

"I want to see Lion's manor at Yonkers for myself," he had explained to Melrosa. "The reports from his agent that Mr. Jay showed me are more than satisfactory. Still, the master's boot is missing from the land, never the most highly satisfactory state of affairs. I prefer to see it at first hand. Besides, I understand that there is good land to be had in the area—some of the confiscated Tory estates. I would like to look around for myself."

Melrosa was sitting on a kitchen stool, wrapped in a big apron, polishing a set of new silver coffee spoons. Her body became very still.

"Do you mean," she asked after a noticeable pause, "that you are thinking of buying a permanent home here for yourself?"

"Yes."

"What about your property in England?"

"I don't believe in absentee landlordship. If I stay on in the States, I will sell it."

"Why?"

"I just told you. I don't believe in—"

"Oh, damn and blast!" she interrupted impatiently. "Not *why* that. I meant *why* would you plan to stay?"

"Take one good guess," he advised her, annoyed and impatient in turn.

"I haven't the faintest notion."

"Haven't you really?" he said in a bored disdainful voice as he sat on the edge of the table and lifted her chin to stare into her unblinking defiant eyes. "You are growing to be as adept a liar as Amalie."

Melrosa slid down from the stool and turned to confront him.

"Amalie! Amalie!" she stormed. "Always that comparison. If it's not one of them, then it's the other. Don't you ever—*won't* you ever see me? Me, Melrosa. And as though it's not enough"—she kicked the stool for emphasis—"to contend with my sisters in your life, I am matched against my own husband and son. Frederick, your cousin, and Lion, who looks like the perfect De Lacey.

"All right, I was pretending, or, if you insist, lying. You're thinking of buying an estate, settling here. That means," she laughed scornfully, "you are also thinking of marriage. So who more suitable than I? Except for one minor matter—you haven't considered or consulted my feelings on the subject."

—She crossed her arms over her heaving breast. "I don't wish to be married because you were madly in love with one of my sisters or shared a wild night of passion with the other. Oh, yes, I know all about it. Sisters talk, you know, and Julianne and I were very close.

"Frederick brought you across an ocean to take care of me; he practically hand-picked you for me himself. I wouldn't even have to change my name again. And Lion adores you and looks enough a De Lacey to be taken for your own son.

"All very neat and perfect," she finished bitterly. "Except, what about me? Maybe I don't want to be married to my husband's plan or for my son's pleasure. Maybe I object to being held in a man's arms because I remind him of one or the other of my sisters. When you look at me and see just *me,* want just *me,* then you may talk to me of this again. Mind you, it doesn't mean that I'll say yes, only that I will consider the subject then."

Alexander had remained calm throughout this outburst. "It may have escaped your attention," he pointed out blandly when she was finally done, "but I happen *not* to have solicited your hand in marriage. Is this a quaint new custom in America," he went on with the utmost courtesy, "declining before you are even asked?"

"You know *damn* well," Melrosa retorted heatedly, "that you *are* planning to have—to take—well, to ask me," she finished in some confusion.

He made no gentlemanly attempt to pretend that his roars of laughter were not directed at her. "You are so good for me, Melrosa," he said finally, wiping away the tears of merriment. "I have laughed more since being in New York with you than for I-don't-know-how-many years. For that pleasure alone," he teased her mercilessly, "I would gladly *have*—or *take*—or *ask* you. And yes, you are correct," he continued mockingly. "At the right time—I know as well as you that the time is not yet—I intend to do all of those things."

"All by yourself?" she taunted him. "May I remind you again that it takes two to make a marriage, including, in this case, my consent?"

"Don't worry, Melrosa." The humility in his manner and the forbearance in his voice were both so patently false she longed to hit him. "There will be two in my marriage bed, and you," he promised gently, "will be one of them."

At this she gave him as panicked a look as ever he had received years ago from the young Melrosa. Blushing violently and visibly, from the exposed skin at her bodice all the way to her hair line, she jumped up, tripped over the rungs of her stool, righted herself before he could reach out a hand to help her, and fled the room without looking back.

They did not meet again until the third week in April when he came back from his tour of inspection.

He returned to a city boiling over with excitement, for on April seventh a courier had been dispatched to Mount Vernon in Virginia with the formal announcement that General George Washington had been unanimously elected to the office of President of the United States. The Commander-in-Chief would be arriving in New York shortly to take up his honors and obligations to his new country.

Alexander De Lacey, late of the forces which had unsuccessfully tried to bring Washington down in defeat, was only mildly interested in this history-making event. The General might come to New York or stay in Virginia with his right good will. Close to three weeks of solitary travel had convinced him surely and for all time, that there was only one person whose presence in New York was of any great moment to him.

The face peering back at him from a cracked mirror, as he shaved on the Sunday morning just after his late-night arrival, softened into a smile. Perhaps, two persons. Melrosa's son, so much a De Lacey, so like his own nephews but with a curious mixture of his father's steadfast gravity and his mother's unquenchable spirit, had become quite dear to him, too.

He arrived at the house on Great George Street at what any fashionable Englishman would consider an incredibly early hour, only to be told by Mary that her mistress had already gone out.

"It's a shame, sir," Mary sympathized. "You missed her by a bare five minutes. I watched the carriage turn the corner, then I went upstairs to put on my bonnet for church. I had just come down to leave when your knock sounded."

"And a very lovely bonnet too," Alexander lied manfully, with an unblinking look at the great black silk calash tied under her chin. "Did Mrs. De Lacey go to church, too, Mary?" he added hopefully. "Perhaps I could join her there."

"Oh, no, sir, she's taking a ship across to Long Island."

Alexander's spirits plummeted. She might be gone all day. Perhaps several days. "Is she visiting friends?"

"Oh, no, sir. She'll be back by tea time. Perhaps, before. It's her first pilgrimage of the spring," she explained simply.

Alexander stared at her blankly. "Pilgrimage?"

"Come spring, until we go to Lacey Manor, and in the autumn, when we get back from Turtle Bay, as long as the weather permits, she goes once a month, faithful as can be. That's the name she calls it, a pilgrimage."

"I'm afraid I still don't understand."

"Your people, sir," Mary told him firmly, though with no disrespect, "they buried them there on the banks of Long Island, the prisoners who died on the *Jersey*."

Alexander's lips tightened. The plight of the

captured Americans aboard the floating prison hell-ship *Jersey* had been felt as a disgrace, long before the postwar horror stories leaked out, to everyone who wore the British uniform. Even so . . . Melrosa . . .

"But why does *she* go?"

"She takes flowers, sir, armsful of whatever flowers are in season, evergreens and ferns, if there are any, and sweet herbs, too, always some bits of rosemary for remembrance."

He said again, strangely troubled, "I still don't understand."

Melrosa's war had not taken place in New York; she had sat it out at Turtle Bay. She had not been concerned with soldiering or prisoners but only the battle in her own mind, as she tried to come to terms with a life that was more than just escape from harsh memories.

"To go all these years," he persisted. "Surely she must have a reason."

It was as though a shutter had been drawn. Mary's face became a perfect blank, and her voice unwontedly formal, like a good servant's. Mary, who was far from considering herself a servant!

"I'm sure I couldn't say, sir. You would have to ask the mistress."

He nodded acceptance of this putdown and asked equably, "Do you know where she boards the ship?"

Mary wasn't quite sure. "It's at Mr. De Lacey's old dock, usually, if it's one of them merchant ships. Other times, she goes by fishing boat. Jem waits for her on the New York side in the carriage."

His face cleared. "Fine. I'll go up and down the docks till I find Jem and send him home." He smiled disarmingly. "*I'll* bring Mrs. De Lacey."

"Whatever you say, sir," Mary returned woodenly, having obviously not forgiven him for his unspecified act of omission or commission.

"May I drop you off at church, Mary?"

"Oh, you shouldn't trouble, sir." She looked longingly out to the street at his fine new carriage.

"It wouldn't be a trouble at all. I shall no doubt be waiting at the dock for an hour or more."

"Then, thank you very much, sir, I'll come right along with you now," Mary offered, completely thawed, and hopeful some of her friends were peering out of nearby windows to see her handed up into the carriage like some grand lady by a man who was brother to a lord.

Good fortune was with Alexander. Having deposited Mary at North Dutch Church on William Street, he turned towards the dock area and was lucky enough to spot Jem ten minutes after he arrived there.

Accepting gratefully the coin pressed into his hands as well as Mr. De Lacey's instructions for him to "get along home," Jem whipped up the horses and got along gladly. He, who could clean up the horses' stalls while whistling cheerily, had always detested the sewage smell of the water and the tedium of the dockside wait.

For Alexander, standing staring out towards Wallabout Bay, where the rotting, stinking *Jersey* had once lay anchored, the time was all too short as he tried to understand the enigma that was his French Rose.

Melrosa, his new love, his last love. Melrosa, so utterly dear, but complex and confusing, in that so like her otherwise unlike sisters.

"Here it comes, sir," said a seaman working on the dock, who had earlier answered some of his inquiries.

Alexander watched the white speck on the horizon come closer and closer until it was clearly seen as a neat, medium-sized vessel.

He read aloud the name painted in black letters on the bow. *The Three Sisters*. Named, no doubt, by Frederick, but with such constant reminders, how was he ever to forget?

The next moment Melrosa was climbing over the ship's side and down onto the dock with the outstretched hands of two seamen from *The Three Sisters* to help her.

She was shaking out her sober gray skirts and looking about for Jem when Alex came up behind her. "Good morning, Melrosa."

"Alexander! Good Heavens! What a surprise! What on earth are you doing down here?"

There had been an instant of pure joy on her face when she said his name, ended like a candle snuffed out, as she broke into banal exclamations and resumed shaking and brushing at her clothing.

"Waiting for you," he said cheerfully. Then he clasped her hands to keep her still. "Do stop twittering," he suggested kindly. "It's not like you."

He continued to hold her with one hand while his other pushed up her chin so he could examine her face. "You've been crying," he observed. "Was there someone special to you on the *Jersey*?"

"Yes," she whispered.

His hands came away from her and clenched at his sides. Was this the simple mystery of Melrosa—a lost lover she had mourned all through the years?

"Is he buried on Long Island?"

"*He!*" Melrosa repeated chokingly. "He! Hundreds of them were buried in the mud on the banks of the river, *thousands*. No graves dug, just the shallow layer of the top shoveled off so they could be dumped just below the surface. When the tides went out, arms and legs and later the bare bones stuck up. Often the river took them, and those that didn't wind up on the banks like refuse floated out to sea to feed the fishes."

"Is that what happened to your friend?"

"Probably. We don't know. She just disappeared."

"*She!*"

"C—a girl we all grew up with, Amalie and Julianne and me. She worked with Amalie's group in New York during the British occupation on the condition—which was honored—that her true name never be revealed. She worked as a number, was condemned as a number and died as a number."

"I don't recall hearing anything about this," Alex said in puzzlement, "and I was close to the intelligence sources."

She didn't answer until they were seated inside the carriage with the coachman carefully traversing the dangerously-rutted road away from the docks. "Are you really interested in all this ancient history?" she asked then.

"So ancient," he said dryly, "that you go on seasonal pilgrimages and come back with tear stains still on your face."

Melrosa shrugged. "Very well, then. She—our friend—was arrested the same day as the tailor Hercules Mulligan."

"My God! I was in the troop that arrested Mulligan, a charming rogue if there ever was one. I heard later in England—and was thankful that he got off; but I never heard anything about a woman spy, other than Amalie."

"I think they probably didn't mean you to. After Amalie"—she smiled a bit apologetically—"your general knew you were loyal, of course, but your discretion may have been a bit suspect. You probably never knew they were interrogating her, and I am sure Sir Henry Clinton"—her voice grew suddenly hard and firm—"carefully omitted to inform you that he had not bothered with a trial for Amalie's friend but sent her straight to the *Jersey*."

Alexander took off his beaver hat and flung it on the seat, running a distracted hand through his hair. "Sweet Jesus!" he said sickly.

"Major André was amply avenged, I assure you," Melrosa told him bitterly. "Hanging would have been the kinder fate."

He glared at her. "Do you think that's what I wanted, revenge for André? André was a soldier; he knew what he was doing and took his chances."

"I'm sorry," Melrosa apologized stiffly. "I shouldn't have said that. She—and Amalie—they knew what they were doing and took their chances too."

Seeing the stern look still bent on her, she essayed a small smile and said again, holding out her hand, "I'm sorry, Alexander."

He accepted the hand and held it tightly in his, even while his feelings were divided between the urge to kiss her and the urge to kick her, just as it had been with her sisters long ago.

This was the moment when he had planned

to say, "I love you and only you. Will you marry me, Melrosa?"

Now he could not.

He did want her for his wife, more than anything on this green earth, he wanted that. And he did love her. Oh, God, how he loved her!

But did he love *only* her? Were her sisters completely out of his heart? It was the bride price she would demand of him, he knew.

Amalie and Julianne might be sweet, fading memories, but unhappily they were not faded enough. Not enough for him and certainly not enough—God help them both!—for Melrosa.

They looked at each other uncertainly over the barrier of their unspoken words and thoughts and feelings.

Chapter Twenty-four

New York, May 1789

... His hair was powdered and worn in a queue behind.
The clothes which he wore were of American manu-
facture . . . the subscribers to the Dancing Assem-
bly gave a ball and entertainment in his honor . . . which
has come to be called the Inauguration Ball . . . the
President is said to have danced with Mrs. Peter Van
Brugh Livingston, Mrs. Alexander Hamilton, and Mrs.
James Homer Maxwell . . .

> *The City of New York
> in the year of George Washington's
> Inauguration, 1789*
>
> *—Thos. E. V. Smith,
> written for the 1889 Centennial*

ALEXANDER AND LION HAD FALLEN INTO THE
habit of a daily hour of talk and play together
after tea time. "Our man's time," Lion called
it proudly.

The last Friday in April, when "man's time" was over and Lion had been sent away to do his lessons, Alexander went in search of Melrosa. He found her in the library with her account books, more than willing to relinquish them to sit and talk with him.

"I've had the most extraordinary invitation," he told her. "It's for the ball being given by your dancing assembly on May the seventh."

"What is so extraordinary about the invitation to a ball?" demanded Melrosa. "I had one, too. I hope you plan to attend and will escort me."

"I don't think I will ever entirely understand Americans. Both invitations seem incomprehensible to me," Alexander protested. "The ball is in honor of the President's Inauguration; he is the guest of honor. Only in America—never in England, were the positions reversed—would a former British officer and the daughter and wife of Tories expect to be invited to such an affair."

"Americans *are* extraordinary," said Melrosa smugly. "That's something you English could never understand. Which is why," she added provocatively, *"we* are now a separate country, and *you* are minus a splendid colony."

"I know of *one* American who stands in danger of being soundly beaten by the British," said Alexander significantly as he pounced.

Laughingly, she eluded his outstretched arms and fled to a far corner of the room.

"Will you escort me to the ball, dear Major De Lacey?" she laughingly wheedled. "I have a lovely new gown to do you credit. It will be my first time in colors other than gray or black or lavender since Frederick died," she added matter-of-factly.

He gave her a courtly bow. "It will be my pleasure to escort you, ma'am. Now come here, you vixen."

"Am I safe?"

"For the present."

She returned demurely to the sofa, only to find her hands seized and held. "But your forfeit is a kiss," he told her.

"Perfidious Albion," she accused.

"*Smart* Albion," he grinned. "Pay your forfeit."

"Do you promise, only one?"

"I promise."

"Very well."

She regarded him soulfully for a moment, then half-crouched, leaned towards him and bestowed a chaste salute on his forehead.

As he made a threatening move, she reminded, "Only one. You *promised*."

"Very well." He leaned back against the sofa. "But I warn you, madame, I will have my revenge when you dance with me at the ball. It is an art I have never really mastered." He played casually with her nearest hand, his fingers stroking up and down her palm, his thumb against the quickening pulse at her wrist. "I must admit I would like to get a glimpse of the great man," he added humorously. "God knows we tried—and failed to during the war. Nevertheless, I still find the invitation extraordinary. I wonder, do you think Mr. Jay had something to do with it? Or do you suppose it's because your President and I are now near neighbors on Cherry Street?"

"Shall we ask him at the ball?" suggested Melrosa flippantly.

"I doubt we shall get the chance. No, no, let us be content, like the planets revolving around the sun, to stand and admire his greatness from afar."

On the night of the ball, Melrosa came down the stairs of Lacey House to find Alexander waiting for her in the hallway. He wore black satin breeches and jacket, white silk stockings, a white satin waistcoat, a large muslin cravat, and buckled shoes. His hair was powdered and tied back in a simple queue.

His eyes glittered strangely in a chalk-white face as Melrosa floated down to him, a vision in celestial blue satin with a white satin petticoat and matching satin heeled slippers. Her neck handkerchief was of Italian gauze with satin border stripes, and a pouf of matching gauze formed the simple headdress on top of her carefully curled and powdered hair. A flowered satin reticule dangled by its velvet strings from one hand, in the other she carried an elegant little fan of ivory sticks.

"You look very grand, Alexander." She admired him proudly, stopping on the third step so their eyes were level. "And very American."

"Thank you," he said in the low, husky voice of someone who has an obstruction of the throat. "I imitated the gesture of Mr. Washington at his inauguration last week. All my clothing is new and of American manufacture."

She nodded her head in grave acknowledgement and stood there waiting.

"You look—most beautiful, Melrosa," he told her rather desperately.

She came slowly and deliberately down the remaining three steps, so that she had to look up at him with the coquette's smile he had seen so often on another from the stage of the Theatre Royal. "Is something troubling you, Alexander?"

He wanted to rail at her, to stroke her even. *You are troubling me, you witch, you bitch, as well you know! You could not look so like her unless you had purposely contrived it. Is this how you induce me to forget her?*

"The carriage is waiting," he said colorlessly, and took the cloak of velvet blue held out by Mary and draped it around Melrosa's shoulders.

They talked of inconsequential matters during their drive to the Assembly rooms, and the frequent silence between such bits of artificial chatter was the silence of hostility.

As soon as they reached the ball, however, Melrosa was restored to animation, smiling and waving at friends and exchanging greetings with many acquaintances she had not seen during the year of her strict mourning. Time and again she introduced Alexander—ignoring their arch looks as she did so—as her husband's dear kinsman.

If anyone knew that Frederick De Lacey's "dear kinsman" had fought as a British officer during the late hostilities, they most courteously ignored the awkward fact, and although the ball was not, by London standards, a brilliant affair, Alexander could hardly be uninterested in the company pointed out to him by Mr. Jay.

Vice-President John Adams. Baron Steuben. Marquis de Moustier. Governor Clinton. General Knox. Chancellor Livingston. And, of course, towering above them all, in stature as well as in importance, George Washington, President of the United States.

By the time they had danced the cotillion, he had grown more accustomed to Melrosa's face surrounded by Amalie's elegant, powdered coiffure instead of her own golden coronet of braids. He had unbent to the point of talking, and even of laughing, causing her to dare tease, as a movement of the dance brought them close, "So I am forgiven?"

"Forgiven, but it will not be forgotten," he retorted.

When the cotillion ended, they moved slowly through the crowd towards a refreshment table. Before they had arrived there, Melrosa was hailed by a handsome dark young man who made up in dignity what he lacked in height.

"My dear Mrs. De Lacey, how happy I am to see you once again."

He clasped both her hands with the warmth of great friendship, a sentiment that was quite evidently returned. Alexander barely had time to identify the uncomfortable sensation in his stomach as the first faint stirrings of jealousy before Melrosa's introduction made such pangs unnecessary.

"Mr. Alexander Hamilton, Secretary of the Treasury. Mr. Alexander De Lacey, Frederick's cousin from England."

"An honor, sir."

"My pleasure, sir."

Both gentlemen bowed, appraising one another. Then Hamilton returned his attention to Melrosa. "I wanted to request the next allemande with you, but, alas, I have been superseded. His Excellency—rather, I must accustom myself to saying, the President is presently engaged with my wife. However, I have his strict orders that the moment their dance ends, I am to bring you to him."

The three stood chatting together while the music continued, with Alexander again marveling at that strange quality in Americans which made them so deadly in warfare, yet so generous to the defeated.

When the dance was over, Hamilton shepherded them across the room. Despite his lack of stature, all made way for him.

Arrived at the Commander-in-Chief, Melrosa sank low in a curtsey. "We all bid you welcome to New York, Mr. President," she told him with a grace and dignity that filled Alexander De Lacey of Beaumont with an altogether possessive pride. "And thank you" —her smile was a mixture of sparkle and mischief—"for coming once again to your country's aid."

The fine-looking but rather austere features had softened amazingly. The overly majestic manner complained of by the more republican was nowhere in evidence as Mr. Washington's hands reached out to assist her rising.

"Thank you, dear lady. It is a great joy and privilege to greet you again."

Then, to Alexander's astonishment, he brought Melrosa's hand to his lips, not in the manner of a man who likes the ladies—which was very much his reputation—but with every evidence of homage.

"Your Ex—Mr. President, may I present

Alexander De Lacey, my husband's cousin from England, who is presently your neighbor on Cherry Street."

The courtesies of greeting exchanged, the President inquired of Alexander, "You are here on a visit, sir?"

"I plan to settle in New York, Your Excellency, but it is not my first visit. I fought at Long Island in 'seventy-five and I was at the siege of Charleston in 'eighty."

Mr. Washington frowned, not in anger, it appeared, but reflectively. "Ah, De Lacey." His brow cleared. "Aide to Sir Henry Clinton?"

"Why, yes, sir."

"No need to look so astonished, Mr. De Lacey. It was my business to be informed of such matters and the business of others"—he cast a sideways glance at Melrosa—"like this lovely lady's sister to apprise me of what I wished to know."

He turned back to Melrosa. "I will be receiving on Tuesdays and Fridays between the hours of two and three and shall be sadly disappointed if you do not wait upon me then. On Sundays we will not receive, but after Mrs. Washington arrives in the city, I hope that you will sup with us informally on that day. My wife has expressed great eagerness to be introduced to you."

Melrosa acknowledged his kind invitations with gratitude and curtsied once more in acceptance of the President's gracious dismissal as the press of people eager to greet him diverted his attention.

As she and Alexander withdrew, he muttered something below his breath and she laughed at him behind her fan.

"Are you finding Americans extraordinary again?" she bantered as they stood drinking glasses of laced punch.

"No, why should I"—ironically—"when I can just see my own King inviting Amalie to sup with him informally on a Sunday night so he might introduce her to the Queen?"

Melrosa choked over her punch and was glad to be relieved of her glass. In the next instant Alexander Hamilton came to claim his dance, and after him a succession of men, both young and middle-aged, but obviously all delighted to partner her.

Alexander himself did no more dancing. Though several girls, quite pretty in their velvets, silks and muslins, cast wistful looks at the tall figure standing at the sidelines, he did not trust himself with anyone but Melrosa in the structured contre dances of New York. Those same pretty girls, though initially glad of a partner, would be sadly chagrined when he started turning wrong or trod on their tender satin-covered toes.

No, he was quite content to stand and watch his French Rose, full of grace, sparkling up at her partners, but with her glance returning ever and again to him.

Chapter Twenty-five

New York
Turtle Bay, 1789

I have heard it asserted that the same sort of handwriting
often prevails in a family; and where the same master
teaches, it is natural enough.

—*Emma*
by Jane Austen

THE BALL WAS OVER AND A FLUSHED, EXCITED
Melrosa had been safely escorted back to
Great George Street. Alexander De Lacey was
standing at his own parlor window with the
curtain lifted, watching as the President's
coach halted a few doors away on Cherry
Street, and the tall, upstanding figure that
could only be George Washington stepped
down into the street.

When he went upstairs, MacDowell was stirring up the fire in the sitting room that adjoined his bedchamber. He cast a shrewd glance at his master.

"Did you no' enjoy the ball, Major?"

"Interesting was the word for it, MacDowell, most interesting. I met the President of the United States as well as a number of other important men in this land. And all of them treated me with the greatest respect, not to say, cordiality."

As he cleaned off his hands and helped relieve his master of his jacket, MacDowell grunted, which Alexander took to mean he was not impressed.

"I found it even more strange," continued Alexander as he walked towards the bedroom, untying his cravat, "that their attitude to me seemed to stem from what they felt towards Mrs. De Lacey. Her father was undoubtedly a Tory, and Cousin Frederick, too, yet there was more than mere admiration for a lovely woman in the way they treated Melrosa. They were respectful —reverent even. Yes, that's the word, *reverent*."

He raised his voice. "Pour a nightcap for us, MacDowell."

When he came back to the sitting room, with his shirt sleeves rolled up, two glasses of brandy were waiting.

Alexander lifted his glass. "To the President of the United States," he toasted lightly. "I think he may have provided me the beginnings of an answer to a puzzle."

He sank down in the nearest of two big armchairs before the fire, indicating that MacDowell was to take the other. Both slouched in their chairs and stretched out their legs with the ease of long habit.

They sipped in companionable silence for a while.

"It's all beginning to make sense," Alexander said in a strange strained voice. "The spying. *The Three Sisters. All* three sisters. They must all have been involved in it. Amalie in New York—Melrosa at Turtle Bay. She was either never mad at all or she got started after her mind was cured. And she could never have participated without Julianne's being aware."

He set down his empty glass and struck his knee, whistling soundlessly. "Good God, Cousin Frederick would have had to know too. He may even have been their leader. What an opportunity! Host to Sir Henry Clinton, and to General Howe before him. Host to all the highest-placed British officers in New York. It was a gold mine for information-gathering. MacDowell, you phlegmatic Scot, you—doesn't anything ever make you look surprised?"

"Plenty, sir," MacDowell said stolidly, "but what you just figured out—no."

"Are you saying you suspected?"

"Aye."

"At the time?"

"No' in the beginning; after I learned about Madame Nostrand, aye."

"And you *said* nothing, *did* nothing."

"Your cousin, the girl you loved, Miss Julianne and Miss Melrosa? What would you have had me do, Major, turn them all in?"

Alexander thought shudderingly of Hale and André and that poor nameless girl on the *Jersey.* "God, no!"

"MacDowell shrugged. "Well, then . . ."

"You should have told me."

The batman eyed the major steadily. "And let you agonize over the decision, sir? I thought my way was better. I knew I had no' such a delicate conscience."

"So you thought I needed a nanny, did you, damn your eyes." He lifted his empty glass. "Where's that brandy?"

MacDowell silently reached behind him for the bottle and poured refills for them both.

Alexander gulped his second, then accepted a third, which went down his throat in a single swallow. With his empty glass held high, he made his toast. "To you, you bloody protective Scot, and to the three sisters, damn all their beautiful blue eyes and lying tongues."

MacDowell took the Major's glass. "Why don't you get to bed, sir? You're looking tired."

"You mean I'm getting foxed, don't you,

nanny? Well, nanny Scot, you may be right."
He got up from his chair, stumbling a little,
and MacDowell reached out a hand to steady
him. "Got to keep my wits about me to deal
with M-Melrosa. Lovely, lying Melrosa. L-
lovely l-lying Am-a-lie. And Jul-ianne with her
golden body. Her body didn't lie that night.
I'd—I'd stake my l-life on that," he said thickly. "MacDowell, you're right, I'm foxed. No
gentleman talks about his lady—ladies fair."

Saying which, he swayed his way to bed to
sleep soundly till almost noon when MacDowell woke him by opening the blinds and letting
in the sun.

Alexander, with the sun stinging his eyelids, began to curse quite heartily.

"Mrs. De Lacey's man delivered a message," MacDowell interrupted the fluent flow
of blasphemy. "The laddie's school is closed
for a week over an infection, and she and the
boy are packing up to go to Lacey Manor. Do
you or do you no' wish to go with them or
follow later in the week?"

Alexander sat up in bed, instantly alert.
"Say that again more slowly."

"There's an infection in Master Lion's
school," repeated MacDowell with exagge-
rated care. "So he and the mistress are going
to Lacey Manor, and you are invited."

"Lacey Manor," Alexander said aloud nos-
talgically. Lacey Manor. If ever there was a
place to get the truth out of Melrosa, then it
was there.

"What time are they leaving?" he demanded.

MacDowell went downstairs to ask Jem, and when he came back, Alexander was already clad in his new buckskin breeches and searching through his drawers for a shirt.

"Within the hour."

"Good." Alexander slammed a drawer shut. "Instruct Jem to tell Mrs. De Lacey that I will be there by then to take up Lion and her. You can follow in the carriage with Jem and anyone else she plans to bring plus the luggage."

"She'll object to arrangements no' of her own making," MacDowell predicted gloomily.

"She may object all she wants so long as she's ready. Just tell Jem."

MacDowell left the room, muttering audibly, "High-handed, that's what you are, high-handed, the two of you."

Alexander laughed aloud in sheer pleasure as he continued dressing. Lacey Manor. Dear God, but it would be good to be there again.

Later that day as his carriage rolled through the entrance gates and along the broad driveway flanked by rows of aged oaks, his heart speeded up in excitement. Beside him, Lion wriggled with equal pleasure.

"We're here," he crowed rapturously. "We're home."

"Yes, we're here," said Alexander more calmly, feeling just like Lion. This—*this* was home.

The first thing he noticed when he entered

the drawing room was a huge portrait of Frederick over the mantel. Not a remarkably skilled portrait but a true-to-life one. Frederick in his favorite old burgundy velvet jacket, with the long clay pipe in his hands, and a typically twinkling smile on his face.

Alexander stood in front of the painting and said over his shoulder to Melrosa, standing just behind him, "I remember Cousin Frederick's telling me the first time I came to Lacey Manor that there was no need for a portrait of him since he had no wife to be delighted by one nor children to point to it proudly."

"It was done by a journeyman painter in the first year of our marriage when he knew there would be a child," said Melrosa huskily.

He turned and saw her staring up at the painting with tear-filled eyes. "You gave him reason to change his mind," he told her gently. "You should be glad and proud, my dear."

"He was so good," said Melrosa with a last tender look at the portrait as they left the room. "I think he was the finest man I have ever known."

The fact that he knew it to be true did not lessen the pain of her words for Alexander even as he felt shamed for feeling jealousy of the dead man who had cherished her and despised himself for begrudging his cousin both a son and those precious few years with Melrosa.

At breakfast the next morning Lion was wild to go outdoors, and Alexander went with him. Melrosa excused herself on the score of too many household matters to attend to.

In the afternoon Alexander said regretfully that he must do some work on the estate books while he was here, and Melrosa, hushing Lion's vigorous protests, led the way to the small office that Frederick had used.

"I think you'll be comfortable at his desk." Her hand unconsciously caressed the shabby upholstered back of her husband's old chair. "The most recent account books are in the right-hand drawer and the older ones here in this back cupboard. All the estate ledgers are stacked on the book shelves and, if you need them, you will find extra candles in this wooden caddy."

He pored over the current account books for at least two hours before getting up to stretch his legs and rub the aching spot at the back of his neck.

Idly he strolled over to the book shelves and took down one of the estate ledgers. It fell open in his hands, and he started chuckling softly as he read aloud.

22 September 1785

An order placed this day with Jos. Barnes, Silversmith, for a set of painted pewter soldiers representing the Fifth Regiment of Foot, the Regiment originally formed in Holland, which served in America during the late Hostilities: to be

sent as a christening gift for Henry Richard, the new little heir to Edward De
Lacey, Earl of Beaumont . . .

Alexander smiled, remembering the fuss at
Beaumont the day the excitingly original gift
arrived from America . . .

He went through the rest of the book, skim-
ming over the purchases of sheep or sales of
wheat, smiling at the frequent hymns of
praise to his small son, sighing over Frederick's matter-of-fact mention of his impending
death, choking a little when he came upon the
words meant for Melrosa on the third of September 1787 . . .

Forgive me, my love, and try to understand that in my Mans Vanity, I wanted
to be that many months longer the one at
the Helm you looked to. All too soon it
may be the other way Round . . .

They were more like journals than estate
ledgers, Alexander thought, with Frederick's
personal reflections and family concerns all
jumbled together with tenant farm reports
and the quality of the new chicken feed.

He returned reluctantly to the less interesting desk work but had barely sat down when
he rose from his chair again, sending it crash-
ing against the wall in his hurry to get back to
the estate ledgers.

They might contain the answers to all his questions; they might help him in his quest.

For twenty minutes he pulled volume after volume off the shelves, checking the dates in every one. They began in the early sixties and continued after Frederick's death. The only gap—and it was a large one—involved the years of the war, from 1777 to 1782.

Melrosa's arrival in '76 was mentioned, and later there were sad entries concerning her "sickness of the mind." The entries continued till December of that year, and then there was nothing. Half a volume of blank pages and no more books until 1782.

It convinced Alexander more than ever before that his theory was right. A four-year interruption of a twenty-year habit at just the time when Amalie and—yes, it had to be—Melrosa and Julianne and Frederick, too, were engaged in intelligence work against the British. Naturally, Frederick would not—in the event of suspicion—wish to condemn them by his own hand.

Just to be sure, at tea time he questioned Melrosa.

"Some of the ledgers are missing?" she repeated. It was one of her more irritating habits that he had noticed before, the parroting of his own words to gain her that few seconds' extra time. A trick, like the bewildered widening of her eyes when she was about to come up with a thundering lie.

"Frederick always kept them on the book shelves, as far as I know," she said, which, no doubt, was true.

He smiled grimly as Melrosa passed him his tea cup. Her hand, he noted, was entirely steady, but then, why not? She was a veritable mistress of deception.

"I have so many boxes of Frederick's things put away," she told him vaguely. "Perhaps they'll turn up somewhere else."

They sat and smiled at each other and sipped their tea and talked, and both their smiles hid a grim determination . . . Melrosa's, to make sure the ledgers stayed safe behind the library panel until the time for concealment was over; Alexander's, to find the blasted books, if they existed, even if it meant searching the house from cellar to attic and tearing up every stick of furniture in Lacey Manor.

That night, when he went up to bed, instead of taking a book from the library, he brought along the estate ledger begun by Melrosa in 1788, more than five months after Frederick had died.

The very first entry brought a lump to his throat.

As I knew would have been my dear husband's wish, I placed an order with Jos. Barnes, Silversmith, for a set of painted pewter soldiers of Fraser's Highlanders, to be sent to England as a chris-

tening gift for Edward James, fourth son
of the Earl and Countess of Beaumont.

He sat by the fire and read on for about an
hour. Like Frederick, she intermingled stories
of Lion with lists of sales and purchases or
acounts of repairs to tenants' roofs. Unlike
Frederick, she did not reveal her thoughts or
feelings.

But then, when did she ever?

She might pretend to be frank and open and
free of care, but that was just the mask she
presented to the world. Behind the mask lay a
shuttered soul.

He got up and walked about the room, with
the big ledger still held in his hands. Something was nagging at him . . . something was
there at the back of his mind. The answer was
within his grasp in something he had just
thought or said. If only . . . if only . . .

He began, in his mind, to go over his own
words, and then suddenly, exultingly, repeated one of them aloud. *"Mask!"*

His pocketbook lay on the dresser, one com-
partment well-stuffed with American bank
drafts, the other containing only a single large
sheet, folded across in eight, as it had been for
all these years. He had carried it always,
never needing to read it after the first few
months. The words were engraved in his
brain and on his heart. As he unfolded it now,
the worn paper cracked and tore slightly at
the folds.

My dear Alexander,
What is there left for me to say now that you have been Informed what you must think is the Worst of me? I used you, yes. I Deceived you, True. But I . . .

He read on, the sudden pain almost as fierce as it had been the first time. Ah, here it was . . .

You wear a uniform and fight for your country. I wore an actor's Mask and fought for mine.

Masks. They had all of them worn masks.

The ledger lay open on the bed where he had tossed it. He had had one great moment of enlightenment. Suddenly, with the evidence before him, there was another.

He sat down on the bed and spread Amalie's letter next to a page of the ledger written in Melrosa's hand.

The sight made him draw in his breath with a hiss.

It was understandable that sisters, perhaps taught by the same master, might write in quite similar fashion. Inconceivable that their hands should be identical! The curling loops of the *y*'s, the lifted tops of the *t*'s, the height of the letters, the slope, the very spacing. No, they were too alike.

They had to have been written by the same person!

286

Amalie and Melrosa. Melrosa and Amalie. "Oh, my God!" he said aloud. "It cannot be."

There was a light tap on the door, and he strode forward and jerked it open.

He blinked once, twice. She stood there in her flowing, flowered dressing gown.

"I heard you moving about." Her voice was soft, apologetic. "I thought, perhaps—" She did not finish, just held out the steaming mug of cider.

Apples and cinnamon and Julianne's unexpectedly exquisite body golden in the firelight. Sweat and salt tears and sticky sweet kisses.

Julianne and Melrosa. Melrosa and Julianne.

A few minutes later, MacDowell, shaken roughly awake from the sound sleep of good conscience, reached swiftly under the pillow for his dirk before a lifted candle revealed the Major's face.

"MacDowell."

"Sir." He bounded up, bare-bottomed, grabbing for his breeches. "Is there some trouble?"

"No. Get back under the covers, man. I'm sorry to disturb you; there was something I had to know."

MacDowell shook his head vigorously, trying to clear his brain.

"What is it, sir?" he asked thickly.

"Tell me, in all the times we came to Lacey Manor during the war, did you ever—even once—think carefully—see Miss Melrosa and Miss Julianne together?"

MacDowell passed a hand across his face, seemingly deep in thought.

"No, sir, I never did," he announced finally.

"Think, man, are you *certain*?"

"Very certain, sir. I never once did." Then he took Alexander's breath away, confirming his incredible suspicion. "How could I, Major?" he asked simply. "How could anyone?"

Chapter Twenty-six

Turtle Bay, 1789

A Jug of Wine, a Loaf of Bread—and Thou
Beside me singing in the Wilderness—

— *The Rubáiyát of Omar Khayyám*

LION CAME TEARING INTO THE BREAKFAST PAR-
lor, where his mother and Alexander had just
sat down to table.

"Mama, MacDowell and I are going to go
exploring. Can we take the pony cart and go
through the woods? And have a basket of
lunch because, after we explore, we will go
fishing on the river?" He stood on one leg and
hopped up and down. "Please, Mama, please
say yes. MacDowell says you have to say yes
or he won't take me."

"Yes," said Melrosa, laughing, "if you promise to do whatever MacDowell tells you."

"I promise *on my honor*," Lion pledged impressively as he scuttled towards the door.

"Come back here and eat your breakfast."

"I have to tell Mrs. Wister about a lunch basket."

"*After* breakfast. I may lack MacDowell's fascination," she told her son sweetly, "but you have to obey me, too, if you want to go exploring."

Lion slid into his seat at the table and cast Melrosa a reproachful glance.

"It is not my fault if I vomit!" he told her with vast dignity.

"Lionel!"

"Well, you told me yourself, Mama, that time I ate the fruitcake after all the apples, if a boy eats when he's already full he will feel sick and vomit. And I'm quite stuffed so—"

"You may be excused," Melrosa interrupted hastily. "Go tell Mrs. Wister."

Lion leaped up from his chair and bounded out of the room, his "'Scuse me," floating back to them.

Melrosa turned to Alexander. "A fine help you were, sitting there with that silly smile on your face."

Alexander said, poker-faced, "I hardly felt I could contradict him. After all, it has been my experience, too, that overeating can cause one to v—"

"Alexander!"

"Your small son," he told her, grinning, "should join the military. His strategy was masterly."

Melrosa could not help joining in his laughter but grimaced as Mary set a plate of ham and eggs before her.

"He has also managed to destroy any appetite I may have had." She pushed back the plate distastefully.

Alex eyed his own full plate without too much enthusiasm. "Why don't we take a leaf from *Sir* MacDowell's book and young Lion's?" he suggested casually. "Perhaps Mrs. Wister could prepare a second basket of lunch."

Melrosa said dutifully, more than a touch of longing in her voice, "I have so much work in the house to get caught up on."

"And I," acknowledged Alexander, "should definitely spend the day at Frederick's desk going through the records. But I have just come home to Lacey Manor, and spring is here, so"—he held out his hand across the table and smiled at her with disarming tenderness—"so let us this one day be wastrels and go picnic by the river."

Melrosa, with her hand still held and crushed in his, succumbed without further coaxing.

"I'll go see Mrs. Wister," she said, recovering possession of her numbed fingers.

"And I, if you permit," said Alexander, "will choose a bottle of wine from Frederick's cellar."

They went down the narrow stairs in single file, Melrosa heading for the kitchen, where Lion's excited voice could still be heard, Alexander turning towards the storeroom.

Three-quarters of an hour later, when Lion skipped importantly down the steps, Mrs. Wister's basket knocking against his knees, Melrosa was upstairs changing her flowered muslin overskirt for an older, less flimsy gown.

"Remind me next quarter to increase your salary," the Major told his man as he lifted Lion up into the pony cart beside MacDowell.

MacDowell winked. "I'm unlikely to forget, sir."

As they exchanged understanding, conspiratorial smiles, the cart moved off with Lion shouting shrilly, "Good-bye, Cousin Alexander." His Cousin Alexander, bounding almost as joyfully as Lion, took the Manor steps two at a time on the way to change his own clothes.

Prudently the Major had sent Jem ahead with the second of the lunch baskets and two of the furry carriage rugs to sit on. "Leaving," as he told Melrosa, eyes gleaming, "my hands free for more important things."

They came to the end of the long walk and passed through the gates that led away from the herb garden and down to the duck pond. "To illustrate," Alexander told her gravely and took both her hands and swung her around to face him.

Melrosa looked nervously over her shoulder. "Someone will see us."

"I am not compromising you, Melrosa, merely holding your hands." He reversed them in his. "Lovely, lovely hands," he murmured. "Amalie's were like velvet; she always wore gloves to protect them, and Julianne's were a bit work-roughened, like a good Dutch hausfrau."

As she pulled her hands free, he saw a flash of anger in her eyes and smothered a smile.

"Shall we continue our walk?" she asked coldly.

"By all means."

They walked, without talking, side by side, yet far apart, till presently they came to a barren spot among the trees where a huge spire-shaped boulder overlooked the river.

"Do you remember this spot, Melrosa?" he asked her huskily.

"Remember?"

"The first time I ever saw you . . . it was here. I had followed your singing, and I couldn't find you. Then I came back and found you standing just there—in your shift— gobbling down my apple pie."

"Yes, I remember now." Melrosa moistened her lips. "I was—frightened. The uniform. But you were—you were very kind."

He reached out to take her hands again, both of them, to swing her around to him as he had done before. She had no wish nor will to protest.

"I thought you were a fairy child," he told her fondly. "A beautiful, bewitching fairy child."

Her trance ended. "A beautiful, bewitching fairy child," she repeated mockingly. "You always were a romantic, Major De Lacey. I was a mad sad raped child, that's what I was!"

"My darling," he said so tenderly that she could not bear it, "you were both."

She gave him the panicked look of the young Melrosa, tore her hands away from his and fled across the grass and through the trees, not stopping till she came to the banks of the duck pond, where Jem had deposited their picnic basket. It sat squarely in the middle of a checked linen cloth with a fur rug from the carriage on either side.

Alex came up behind Melrosa, put his hands on the rigid shoulders, and turned her around to him. There were tears tangled in her lashes. Lightly, lovingly, he kissed the tears away.

"I saw you dance here that same day, Melrosa. Frederick and I stood on the other side of the bridge and watched you. I had never seen a woman dance like that before, so unrestrained and free. I have never seen anyone but you dance that way since."

He shook his head. "The other night at the ball, I watched and listened to others admiring the way you performed the allemande and the rigadoon, stately and proud, and all I could think of was the girl who had not performed at all but just danced that day with wild beautiful gypsy abandon. That, *that* was dancing! I remembered it always in England. I have wished I could see you dance again."

"Did you? Did you really?"

"Haven't I just said so?"

Melrosa bit down on her lower lip, then suddenly tossed her head high. The tears were gone from her eyes; a wicked smile flashed across her face.

She untied her cloak and flung it down beside the picnic basket. She kicked off her shoes, laughing deep in her throat when Alexander had to grab quickly to keep them from going into the duck pond.

She ran a short distance away, pulling out her pins and combs as she went, letting them fall where they would. She stood on her toes and began to dip and sway, tantalizingly slow at first, then gradually accelerating her movements until she was dancing just as he had remembered. Her stockinged feet seemed barely to touch the grass as she circled around; her hair fluttered like a banner behind her, gold in the sunlight. Every swirling movement was incredibly sensuous.

Then she was running back across the grass to him, dropping beside him, dry-mouthed and breathless, flushed and sweating and still shaken by excitement.

"Oh God, I haven't danced like that in years!" she panted. "I need some water."

"Just wine, I'm afraid," said Alexander, still shaken himself. He uncorked the bottle and poured a glass for her with hands that were far from steady. She drank it like water and promptly held out her glass for another.

She rolled over on her back, looking up at the sky, lifting her head every now and then to take another swallow.

"Oh, my, but that was wonderful!" she said. "*You* were wonderful!"

The head came up. "I was, wasn't I?" she said so smugly he could not help laughing. She finished her drink, and the head slammed down again. "I was the dancer," she said in a slightly slurred voice. "Amalie might be the actress, but me—me—Melrosa—I was the one who could dance."

He came and sat closer to her so that he could look down into the glowing face and fill her empty glass.

She sat up. "You're not drinking with me," she accused.

He half-filled his own glass, but he only sipped, while she swallowed.

"I suppose we ought to eat. Not good—drinking on empty stomach."

"I think, my sweet," he told her, "it's a little late to lock the barn door."

"In that case," said Melrosa, "thank you, I'll have more wine."

She held out her glass, and Alexander poured what was left of the bottle. Then he moved even closer and put an arm around her. "Do you remember our picnic in the carriage?" he whispered. "The day I was trying to get some time alone with you and we took a country drive."

She made a funny bubbling sound in her throat. "You s-scared me to d-death," she hiccuped. "Ch-chomping on that ch-chicken breast and l-l-looking at me as though—exactly as though—"

"Exactly as though I planned to do the same to you."

She sniffed. "And then we fought."

"We always fought, but it never lasted. Remember our other picnic?"

"Don't—don't remember 'nother."

"Of course, you do. It was the night before I went back to England . . . we were on the bed . . . and the cider spilled . . ." His arms were gripping her tightly. He looked down into the blue, blue eyes. "Remember how wonderfully our kisses tasted of cinnamon and apples?"

"Oh, yes," breathed Melrosa, and without further words, flung both arms around his neck, her upturned face and eager lips mutely begging for more of those kisses. The cider flavor was missing, but otherwise it was the same. Kisses that tasted of sweat and salt tears—from both their eyes—and of wine and the passionate joy of reunion.

When their mouths reluctantly parted, he caressed her closed eyes with his fingertips. "Why?" he whispered. "Why, Amalie—Julianne—Melrosa, why?"

The eyes opened; they opened wide in shock. Genuine, not simulated shock.

"Oh Lord!" she gasped. "I hadn't planned to tell you like th-this!"

"As far as I can see, you hadn't planned to tell me at all," Alexander pointed out coldly.

"That's not true."

"In the year 1800, perhaps?"

"W-wh-when you fell all the way in love with j-just me," she quavered. "N-not anything left over f-for them."

"Them?"

"Amalie and Julianne."

"That doesn't make sense!" he shouted. "How can you be jealous of yourself? You *are* Amalie and Julianne."

"I'm not!" She pulled her legs up and hunched over, hugging her knees and weeping bitterly. "I *created* them. They were parts I played. And *you*," she said accusingly, "you fell more in love with those made-up creatures than you ever did with me."

"Melrosa, weren't you playing a part, too?" he asked her, trying to be patient. "The part of the little girl who had gone out of her mind because she was violated?"

"That was *never* a part. Never. That was me, the real me, for six months after it happened. Later on, when we decided to use it, all I had to do was remember how I had behaved before. It was easy when I thought back to—that night." She wiped her face with the back of her hand. "I think it would still be easy."

He handed over his handkerchief, then firmly took both her hands in his. "My darling," he said, "I have been trying to understand you and your supposed sisters for a good ten years. I think Frederick intended you to tell me everything when he asked me to come back to America."

Her tears fell afresh. "Frederick intended you to m-m-marry me," she said on a wail. "That's why he asked you to wait till my year's mourning was over."

"Well, I'm perfectly willing to oblige him," Alexander said reasonably, "but I do think I have a right to know just who it is I'm marrying. Is there really a Melrosa?"

"As a matter of fact, there really are an Amalie and Julianne, too," she sniffled. "My mother's sisters—they used to live with us before the fire in '76. I would have been with them visiting our relatives in Trenton, but I got sick, and my father worried so. I had an older sister Solange who died, you see. Anyhow, I was there and—and—Frederick told you about it, didn't he?"

She started tearing out handfuls of grass. "There were three of them. Two Hessians who smelled of sausage and a British dragoon who smelled like—like burned meat. My father was a—a good man, a really good man. There was no reason for—they threw him into the fire alive, and then they took me away and hurt me and hurt me and hurt me."

Alexander was hurting her, too, his hands holding her shoulders in such a death grip, his fingernails drew blood. She didn't seem to mind or even to feel it.

"I was brought to Uncle Frederick's the next day," she went on, "and I really did go out of my mind a little. I expect it was so much easier *not* to be me. But, gradually, I was"— she shrugged—"all right, and not too long after, I found out that Frederick was not a Tory at all but actively working on the American side.

"I slept badly," she explained, "and often I would come down to the kitchen in the middle of the night to get something to eat. One night when I came down, there was a meeting going on in the estate room next to the kitchen. The men didn't want to trust me; they wanted me sent away to Jersey, for fear I might give them away, but I said I wouldn't go. I said I had as much or more reason than any of them for staying and helping them.

"I didn't, of course," she admitted. "*They* were Patriots, *I* wanted revenge; but over the years it changed. I read and I talked to Frederick and I listened to them all, and in time I came to understand why we risked so much to have our own country.

"I didn't do much at first. Just deliver an occasional message to a peddler. Then it was summer, and all the British officers descended on us for Uncle Frederick's open hospitality. They drank and talked most indiscreetly and every day"—she chuckled— "little mad Melrosa would go running around the place in her shift, but mixed in with all my real flowers were the artificial flowers made out of silk, with written messages sewn inside the petals. I would toss my flowers to men waiting in the fishing boat or sometimes just hand them out to one of the pretended gardeners. Who would ever dream of suspecting me? Did you?"

Without waiting for him to answer, she hurried on, "The only trouble was that little mad Melrosa couldn't attend the lunches and dinners and riding parties, and there were all those talking men, so we decided to invent Julianne, who took care of me *and* the house, too. It gave her a reason for disappearing whenever she had to and for poking and prying in everything. She had an excuse when she was caught in their rooms, and she wasn't attractive, so nobody would much notice her."

Alexander reached up and pulled her onto

his lap. "She was *damned* attractive without any clothes on—how did you make her look so different? How the hell did you make the three of you look so alike and yet so different? You weren't even the same height."

She nestled contentedly against him. "Easy," she said in a sleepy voice. "I was always barefoot, remember? Amalie wore slippers without heels. And Julianne's leather shoes had little wooden lifts added to make her heels even higher. Padding to make Julianne's figure seem straighter, graying powder to dull her hair, and cosmetics to change her skin tone, make the pockmarks and the shape of her nose. When I was first Melrosa, I used cotton binding to flatten my bosom; later I didn't bother. I never worried about my hair; I just let it hang down. That's why Amalie always had hers powdered and worn in curls. And drops to brighten or dull our eyes so they looked different shades of blue.

She yawned and put her hand against his cheek caressingly. "We invented Amalie the next winter when all the British officers stayed mostly in New York. The Triple Ring— our group—thought they were too good a source to give up, so we also invented a reason why Amalie could never come to Turtle Bay or have anything to do with Julianne. One of our men had a—a connection with the Theatre Royal and got me a small part. They wanted me there because my original assignment was to get friendly with André. Our side knew he was deep in intelligence work, but mostly I used him to meet other officers who were more gullible. The rest of what happened was completely unexpected, my making a hit and getting good parts and becoming well known as an actress. But it was good because it helped our work until—"

"Until?"

"Until *you* came, and I had to go on with what I was doing. I just *had* to, Alexander; I believed in it too much. It wasn't easy for me either, allowing you to think—*making* you think I was a—a husband-stealer—from my own sister, too—and living under a rich man's protection; oh, all those horrible things you thought about me. I had to convince you that they were true, and at the same time I was furious because you believed me."

He turned her around on his lap, forcing her to face him.

"In your farewell letter to me as Amalie, you said you loved me, you would always love me. Tell me, Melrosa, who wrote those words, *you* or Amalie?"

"I did."

"Were they true?"

"Yes, Alexander."

"Do you love me now as much as I love you, Melrosa?"

"I don't know how much you love me, Alexander, but I love you with all my heart."

"Oh, God!" he said thickly. "Eight awful weary wasted years." He crushed her to him so tightly she gasped quite happily for breath.

Then he put his hands on her waist and lifted her back onto the fur rug. "We've got to clear up one thing," he told her sternly.

"Yes, sir," said Melrosa, widening her eyes.

He gave her a little shake. "*You* may have created Amalie and Julianne, but they were a part of you, just as you, whether you intended it or not, were very much a part of them. So let's have no misunderstanding now or in the future about who *I* am in love with. The three of you are one, and if I'm in love with that one or all three, it's still *you!*"

"Whatever you say, Alexander."

"Melrosa!" he roared. "I mean it."

She began laughing. Then she wriggled towards the picnic basket. "I'm tired, but I'm hungry too. And thirsty. Is there any more wine?"

"You drank enough, that's why you're tired. Melrosa . . ." He kissed her hands, first one, and then the other. "You did what you thought was right. I did not. I could have offered for Amalie much sooner—I could have asked Julianne that night to go back to England with me. Even if the both of you"—he smiled faintly—"had said no, I would still have less to be ashamed of now."

Melrosa looked at him very straightly.

"I paid dearly for that mistake," he told her. "My own marriage was a disaster. I have no right to begrudge you any happiness you had in yours. Did—You *did* come to love Frederick, did you not?"

"I always loved Frederick; I was never *in* love with him. He knew it, but he was generous in love as in everything else. And though you may find it hard to believe, he was grateful to you."

"To me?"

"For giving him a son," said Melrosa softly.

It took a full minute to sink in. Then his face went pale, and he held out shaking hands to her. Melrosa took them comfortingly in hers.

"Lion?" he croaked. "That wonderful boy—mine?"

Melrosa nodded.

"Is that why you married Frederick?"

"I think that once you were gone, and I got word from England that *you* were married, I might have wed him anyhow," Melrosa answered with painful honesty, "but under the circumstances—well, I told Frederick and we were married six weeks after you left."

She nibbled furiously at her lower lip. "There's something else. I—Frederick—he—he didn't come near my room the whole first year we were married. Fourteen months actually. So, when Lion was six months old, I went to his room. I was prepared to be very noble and self-sacrificing in return for all he had done for me. Much to my surprise, I discovered something I had never known before. I didn't have to sacrifice or be noble at all. He was a—a tender lover and a strong one, and, without being in love with him, being *with* him was very wonderful. We may not have had—rapture, but we had happiness."

She put her arms around Alexander. "I won't mind having rapture again," she whispered.

"I have a son," he said in dazed disbelief. *"You*, and a son."

"He has your name, you will bring him up, but you can't claim him as you might like. He has to remain Frederick's son," Melrosa said firmly. "We both owe Frederick that."

"I don't give a damn how I have him so long as I have him. Besides, you'll give me more, won't you?"

"I expect so,' said Melrosa consideringly. "I got Lion from you rather easily."

He grinned. "Amalie or Julianne?"

She grinned back. "I don't know, square in between."

He stood up and pulled her to her feet. "Come on."

"Come on, where?"

"To find the nearest minister and see about posting the banns."

"That's miles away. I'm hungry," she moaned.

"So am I." He gave her a look that set her knees quaking and sent her temperature soaring. "And the satisfaction of *my* appetite requires a minister."

Melrosa wet her lips. "Mine, too," she whispered, "but—"

"No *buts*."

"But it's a long drive. We can take the picnic basket in the carriage with us. And perhaps" —she smiled lovingly up at him—"perhaps a jug of cider?"

Tapestry

HISTORICAL ROMANCES

Next Month From Tapestry Romances

TURQUOISE SKY
by Monica Barrie
SILVERSEA
by Jan McGowan

POCKET BOOKS

Home delivery from Pocket Books

Here's your opportunity to have fabulous bestsellers delivered right to you. Our free catalog is filled to the brim with the newest titles plus the finest in mysteries, science fiction, westerns, cookbooks, romances, biographies, health, psychology, humor—every subject under the sun. Order this today and a world of pleasure will arrive at your door.

 POCKET BOOKS, Department ORD
1230 Avenue of the Americas, New York, N.Y. 10020

Please send me a free Pocket Books catalog for home delivery

NAME _____

ADDRESS _____

CITY _____ STATE/ZIP _____

If you have friends who would like to order books at home, we'll send them a catalog too—

NAME _____

ADDRESS _____

CITY _____ STATE/ZIP _____

NAME _____

ADDRESS _____

CITY _____ STATE/ZIP _____